Pax DEMONICA

NEW YORK TIMES
BESTSELLING AUTHOR

Julie Kenner

Pax Demonica: Trials of a Demon-Hunting Soccer Mom
Demon-Hunting Soccer Mom, Book 6
By Julie Kenner

Copyright © 2014 Julie Kenner
Print Edition
All rights reserved.
juliekenner@gmail.com
http://www.juliekenner.com

ISBN - 10 - 1940673208
ISBN - 13 - 978-1-940673-20-2

Cover Design and Interior format by The Killion Group
http://thekilliongroupinc.com

OTHER BOOKS BY THE AUTHOR

Kate Connor Demon-Hunting Soccer Mom Series

The Demon You Know (short story)
Carpe Demon
California Demon
Demons Are Forever
Deja Demon
Demon Ex Machina
PAX Demonica

**Learn more at
www.DemonHuntingSoccerMom.com**

USA Today **Bestselling Protector (Superhero) Series**

The Cat's Fancy (prequel)
Aphrodite's Kiss
Aphrodite's Passion
Aphrodite's Secret
Aphrodite's Flame
Aphrodite's Embrace
Learn more at www.WeProtectMortals.com

BY J. KENNER AS J.K. BECK

Shadow Keepers series (dark paranormal romance)
When Blood Calls
When Pleasure Rules
When Wicked Craves
When Passion Lies
When Darkness Hungers
When Temptation Burns
Shadow Keepers: Midnight

AS J. KENNER

***New York Times & USA Today* bestselling Stark Trilogy (erotic romance)**
Release Me
Claim Me
Complete Me
Take Me (eBook novella)

***New York Times & USA Today* bestselling Stark International Series**
Tame Me

***New York Times & USA Today* bestselling Most Wanted series**
Wanted
Heated
Ignited

DEDICATION

To all the wonderful fans of Kate . . . thank you
for your patience!

CHAPTER 1

There were bodies everywhere. Pushing. Shoving. Writhing.

Some malevolent. Others merely . . . existing.

It was hell. Absolute, pure, undiluted hell.

I should know. My name is Kate Connor, and I'm a Level Five Demon Hunter with *Forza Scura*, a secret arm of the Vatican tasked with taking out demons and other nasties. Which means that I'm pretty well-versed in the realities of hell.

And trust me when I say that the Fiumicino Airport in Rome definitely qualifies as one of Dante's seven circles. Especially when you happen to be navigating that hell with a cranky toddler. Although to be fair, said toddler wasn't much crankier than my husband, Stuart, who hates to fly and barely slept a wink on the plane. Not that I slept much either. Frankly, I was a little cranky, too.

"Hungry," Timmy said, plunking himself down on the floor and doing a good impression of a boulder. "Momma, Momma, I hungry."

I had his hand in a vise grip, so when he stopped, I stopped as well, the result being that the two of us created a human dam in the flow of travelers. A chorus of curses surrounded us. English, Italian, French, and at least a dozen other languages I didn't recognize. Rome is nothing if not cosmopolitan.

Behind me, Stuart stopped short, and I felt his fingers close on my shoulder as he steadied himself. "Timothy Allen Connor, do you want to get squashed? Kate, do something."

I grimaced. "Thanks for the tip. Until you said something, my plan was to do nothing at all." Okay, maybe I was more than just a little cranky.

"Don't like squash," Timmy said as I scooped him up and settled him on my hip. "Happy Meal. Want a Happy Meal." His little hand shot out as straight as a compass arrow, and with as much precision too. It pointed right at a McDonald's sitting there pretty as you please in the middle of the concourse. Does the kid have radar or what?

"Oh, gross." Allie, my fifteen-year-old daughter, was a few feet ahead of me and off to the side. I eased that direction as quickly as I could, eager to get away from the crowd that threatened to run me down.

A dark-haired twenty-something male model type eyed me up and down as he pushed past Stuart, his expression smug, as if he knew that the secret to stress-free travel was to wing it alone, and was mocking my foolishness. I recognized his Pepperdine T-shirt and denim jacket from the plane. He'd been sitting three rows up from us and across the aisle, and he'd turned back once too often to look in my daughter's direction. My high school–age daughter's direction.

Allie had pretended not to notice, but she'd checked her hair and lip gloss at least a dozen times during the flight, and when she wasn't staring at an electronic device, she was gazing vaguely in that guy's direction. Call me capricious, but Mr. Pepperdine wasn't on my list of favorite people. Reflexively, I sniffed the air, frowning slightly as I caught a lingering, putrid scent. A demon? The thought that I might be justified in shoving a stick through Mr. Pepperdine's eye cheered me, but the glee passed as quickly as it had come. That wasn't a demon stench I was smelling. Just the aroma of dozens of international travelers in desperate need of a shower.

Nice.

I glanced at Allie to see if she was primping again, but thankfully she hadn't noticed Mr. Pepperdine. Instead, she was leaning against one of the plastic chairs that lined the gate area. Her brand new iPhone was out, her thumbs were flying, and her brow was furrowed in concentration. And why not? She'd just spent over fifteen hours cut off from the world. No phone. No Internet. Nothing but her iPod, her laptop, six magazines, two books, and a half dozen flirtatious glances at a stranger. No wonder she had to immediately text her best friend.

I snapped my fingers in front of her nose and she jumped. "Come on. Time to move. If you don't want french fries you can get a packet of sliced apples." That's the nice thing about fast food. No matter where you are in the world, you know exactly what you're going to get. Not great if you're trying to soak up the local atmosphere, but awesome if you're traveling with kids. And to be honest, I wasn't all that keen on soaking up the airport schtick anyway.

Allie's nose crinkled. "Who knows how long those apples have been in that package? And they're still not brown? That's just not normal."

"Fine. Then have some of your trail mix." Allie changed dietary requirements as often as most people change underwear. At the moment, she was all about whole, unprocessed foods. Since that wasn't something I could argue against, I didn't. But I silently mourned the fate of my grocery budget.

I waved my arm, ushering her toward the golden arches. "Come on. Presumably their water is fresh enough for you. And say goodbye," I added, shooting a stern glance toward the phone. "Your texts are going to cost us a fortune."

She grimaced but quickly tapped out a few letters, then shoved her phone in the back pocket of her jeans. I cleared my throat, and she immediately shifted it to her front pocket. We'd had *the talk* on the plane. No, not that talk; *that* talk was old news. This was the one about Rome and pickpockets and gorgeous dark-haired guys with chocolate eyes just intense enough to make you swoon . . . right before they snatched your purse.

She'd glanced toward Mr. Pepperdine when I'd said that, and I probably should have felt a twinge of guilt. For all I knew, the guy was entirely innocent. Except I didn't believe it. I learned long ago that no one is entirely innocent. And no, that's not a lesson that came from fighting demons. That one comes with parenthood.

"Kate, let's get going." Stuart adjusted his grip on the rolling bags. I shifted thirty-eight pounds of squirming boy on my hip and silently assured myself that the universe would self-correct later.

"Happy Meal?"

"I'm on it, Cowboy."

"Whatever," Allie groused. "Guess the baby wins again." She hoisted her backpack up onto her shoulder and slouched toward the restaurant. I followed, perfectly content with the thought of a Big Mac. I'd eat local later. Right then, I just wanted food and no tantrums. This was supposed to be a vacation, after all. For the most part, anyway. And the less stress, the better.

Stuart, however, was underwhelmed by the prospect of our first taste of Rome. "Seriously, Kate? Look at that line. We've got Goldfish and applesauce in the bag, and he just finished three chocolate chip cookies. The kid will survive until we get to the B&B."

"That's at least an hour away," I said. "Maybe longer." We still had to get our luggage, catch a taxi, and then make the forty-kilometer drive. Father Corletti had offered to send a car from the Vatican for us, but I'd declined. I hadn't been back to *Forza's* headquarters in over fifteen years; I didn't want their first impression after so long to be of blatant crankiness. Mine or my family's.

Stuart didn't look convinced.

I reached for him and twined my fingers with his. "Family time, remember? Taking it easy, exploring Italy, going with the flow." Okay, so that wasn't *everything* I had planned, but considering Stuart was still a little uncomfortable with the whole my-wife-is-a-demon-hunter thing, I figured it was probably best not to work *Forza* or training sessions into the schedule until he'd had at least one good Italian meal. With wine.

Stuart lifted a brow. "Fair enough. But when you said we'd go with the flow, I didn't realize that meant fast food."

"Point taken." Of course, when I said it I also hadn't been sure what I wanted. My original itinerary had included only me and Allie. The last few months had been rough, from both a demon-hunting and a marital perspective, and we were flying back to Rome to visit the town I still thought of as home. I craved the familiarity of my past, and if my parents had been alive, I'm sure I would have been running to them. Instead, I headed to the only family I'd had growing up—*Forza Scura*—and the one person I thought of as a parent, Father Corletti, who'd taken me in when I was orphaned at four.

When I was younger I knew that I could die fighting demons. I'd thought I understood what fear was, but I was wrong. Fear is knowing that your children can be ripped away from you. That the man you love could die or leave you. That your family may well be the first casualty of your war against the forces of evil. I know that fear now. I've touched it. Tasted it. And it's cold and bitter.

But miracles happen every day, cutting a swath through the fear and letting hope grow. Trust me, I know. That whole water-to-wine thing has nothing on Stuart showing up on the doorstep with passports and suitcases and the determination that we were all going to Italy together. That no matter how hard it might have been for him to adjust to my not-quite-as-secret-as-it-used-to-be job fighting demons, he wanted to make it work, and we were moving into the future together. As a family.

His return had twisted up my heart, but it didn't completely soothe my anger. He'd left me—more than that, he'd taken our son. And he'd done that after he knew my secret. After he'd told me that he understood, that he could handle it. After he'd walked away once and returned to supposedly start fresh and new.

I'd told myself that I had to be understanding. That learning your wife is a Demon Hunter is Big News, so how could I fault Stuart for stumbling a bit as we battled the storm?

Yes, he'd come back, and as far as I could tell, he was serious about making our marriage work. About making it stronger. But that didn't soothe the anger that bubbled beneath the surface. And it didn't erase my fear that when it got tough again, Stuart would be gone.

I needed time. I needed trust.

Hopefully, this trip would be both a balm and a cure. Or at least a step in the right direction.

I dredged up a smile and gave Stuart's hand another squeeze. "If you want to get going that badly, I won't argue. But you can be the one to distract him as we walk past. And then explain to him why he's not chowing down on a—"

"Don't say it. You'll just rile him up again."

I laughed. "Oh, come on," I wheedled. "Did he or did he not manage to go an entire plane ride without throwing a tantrum? The kid was an angel. He deserves a treat."

"An angel?"

"Half an angel," I amended as I eased us toward Allie and into the McDonald's line. "And the couple behind us thought he was cute." A fact for which I was supremely grateful. I'm not sure I would have been so gracious if a small child had twice tossed a bedraggled blue bear into my lap. Boo Bear's been in our family since Timmy was five months old, and I—

Shit.

"Kate?" From the concern in Stuart's voice, the panic must have been all over my face. "It's not—I mean, there aren't—*demons?"*

Allie whipped around, yanking her earbuds out as she turned, ready to spring into action. "Demons? Where?" Allie's nothing if not eager. In fact, one of the purposes of the trip was to let her get in some legitimate *Forza* training, a reality that both scares me to death and makes me pretty dang proud.

"That's impossible," Stuart said, and I'm pretty sure I heard terror in his voice.

"Boo Bear?" Timmy must have picked up on our panic. His head swiveled as he searched for his buddy, his face turning redder with each passing moment.

"Hey, baby," I soothed, rubbing his legs.

"Boo Bear!" The name was more like a squall, and his little body trembled. Around us, all the other tourists jonesing for a Mickey D fix started to stare. I slid out of line and edged up against the concourse wall, out of the way of the traveling hordes.

Timmy's wail ratcheted up, as if he was increasing the volume to better fill the space. Helpless, I bounced him and patted his back, saying meaningless soothing words about how we'd find him, and not to worry, and all sorts of other lies. I sounded rational and calm. Inside I was panicking. Two weeks in Italy without the stuffed little bear would not be good.

"Maybe those people took it," Allie said. "The ones the munchkin kept tossing Boo Bear at."

"No way. They were totally understanding."

Allie rolled her eyes. "Yeah, so they said. What were they supposed to do on the plane? Taking the stupid bear is the best way to get revenge."

"When did you become so cynical?" I refused to believe she could be right. "Check the diaper bag," I added, dropping my shoulder so that the bag slid to the floor. Allie crouched down and opened it, then immediately shook her head.

"Maybe you put it in one of the carry-ons," Stuart suggested.

"Why would I have done that? For that matter, you were sitting right beside me. You know I didn't."

"You were exhausted, Kate. Maybe you got fed up and decided that taking the bear away was the best way to make Timmy stop throwing it."

"That actually would have been a great plan," I agreed. "But I didn't do it."

"You're sure?"

I stared him down. He managed not to crumble under the force of my gaze for about thirty seconds longer than the kids usually lasted. Then he caved.

"I'm just saying that you were tired. Maybe when I got up to go to the bathroom, you put the bear away."

"Or maybe you did," I countered as Timmy's wails shot up another ten decibels.

"Maybe it's still on the plane," Allie said.

The kid had a point. "I'll go," Stuart said, and was gone before I could respond. I'm not sure if he was trying to be helpful or just escaping the chaos.

"Well, I'm going to at least check the carry-ons," Allie said as I wondered if we could find a replacement bear on eBay and, if so, how much international shipping would cost.

"Nothing," Allie said a moment later. "But it's got to be around here somewhere. I mean, how can a—"

"Excuse me?" The voice was polite, respectful, and when I looked up and saw Mr. Pepperdine standing beside us holding a bedraggled blue bear, I swallowed the bitter taste of guilt. Apparently not every male who looked at my daughter leaned toward the demonic. "I found this just past the gate. I was on my way to Lost and Found when I overheard you, and—"

"Boo Bear!" Timmy reached for the bear, then hugged his friend close.

"Right," Allie said, springing to her feet and smoothing her hair. "Thanks. We were afraid the little bugger was going to need therapy. He's nuts for the bear."

Mr. P's smile was wide, showing perfect teeth. "My pleasure." His gaze lingered on my daughter for a moment longer than my mom instincts approved of, and despite the fact that he'd stepped in as our savior, I cleared my throat. He turned his attention to me. "You should be careful," he said. "Losing something as precious as that . . . well, it could be dangerous."

Something in the way he said it made my insides twist. I took a step toward him, instinctively edging between him and my kids. "What do you mean?"

But he was no longer looking at me. Instead, he was focused on something over my shoulder. I shifted to glance back, but saw nothing interesting. Just a mishmash of travelers and one lanky maintenance man in tan coveralls with an airport ID badge striding past us. When I turned back, Mr. Pepperdine was stepping away from us.

"Enjoy your trip," he said. "And take care."

And then he disappeared into the crowd, his words lingering along with the faint aroma of rotting flesh.

A tight fist seemed to squeeze my heart, and I shot a glance at Allie to see if she'd smelled it too. But she was simply staring after our potentially demonic savior, her eyes full of gooey teenage fantasies.

Shit.

"Watch your brother," I said.

"Huh?" Her dreamy eyes turned toward me, but I was already hurrying away.

Behind me, I heard Stuart call my name, and I yelled back over my shoulder. "Bathroom! Be right back!" I hoped I would. I hoped I was imagining things. I had to be, right? Because why would a demon talk to me of all people? And why the hell would a demon bother to return a lost lovey?

As it turned out, I wasn't lying about the bathroom. A few yards ahead, I saw my quarry shift left and aim himself toward the men's room. I followed—or I tried to. Another plane had landed, and I was suddenly caught in the flow of emerging passengers, their moving bodies and shifting luggage blocking my view.

By the time I'd pushed my way through the mob, Mr. P was nowhere in sight. But I'd seen where he was heading, and I hurried toward the men's room, determined to rush right in, propriety be damned. Unfortunately, I was stopped short just inches from the entrance by the barrel chest of another maintenance man emerging from the facility. He had a mop in one hand and a candy bar in the other. He bit off a chunk of chocolate and mumbled at me in Italian so garbled I could barely make out vowel sounds.

"Sorry," I said. "I can't understand you."

"Women," he said in English, and he accentuated the word with an outstretched hand pointing to the ladies' room next door.

"No, see, my, um, friend. He's in there. I think he's sick. I need to check on him." I shifted to go around him. He shifted to block my path.

"No enter." He took another bite. "Closed." The candy added an unpleasant smacking sound to his words. "For cleaning."

"It's really important. He might need help."

"Is empty."

"I saw him go in."

"Kate?" I turned to find Stuart behind me. "What's going on?"

"I—" I had no idea what to say. Lie and keep the vacation rolling smoothly along? Tell the truth and admit that I may, possibly, perhaps have seen a demon? A nice, helpful demon who returned missing bears? I ran my fingers through my hair, suddenly flustered. "I thought I saw someone I knew," I said lamely.

"Empty," the maintenance man repeated, then shoved the last of the candy into his mouth. "I do floors." He mimed mopping the floors, looking between me and Stuart. "Is nobody."

"Kate?" There was concern in Stuart's eyes. "Is something wrong?"

"No," I said as I shook my head. But that was a lie. There was no sign indicating that the restroom was closed. The mop head was bone dry. And there wasn't a bucket in sight. I forced a bright smile. "No," I repeated, hoping that my suspicions were wrong. "I thought I saw an old friend, but I must have imagined it." I hooked my arm through his. "Come on," I said. "I think it's time to get this vacation started."

He grinned in reply, and as we headed back to the kids, I forced myself not to look toward the men's room. Maybe I'd been wrong and Mr. Pepperdine hadn't gone in there. For that matter, maybe he wasn't a demon at all. Lots of people had bad breath, especially after hours on a plane. Maybe he just really needed some Listerine.

And maybe I excel at self-delusion.

"Our bags are probably the only ones on the carousel by now," Stuart said, and I realized he was right. Our first adventure in Rome had taken up quite a bit of time.

He threaded his fingers through mine, lifted my hand to his lips, and kissed it. "Have I mentioned how much I love you?"

"Many times," I said, "but feel free to say it again."

"I love you," he repeated. "And this is going to be a great trip. Our first big family vacation," he added, and I realized that he was right. We'd gone to Disneyland when Timmy turned two, but since we live only a few hours north of Anaheim, that wasn't exactly the vacation of a lifetime.

I shook off the lingering sense of foreboding, pausing long enough to kiss my husband. Right then, right there, my first priority was my family. Stuart was right; this trip was going to be amazing.

Happy Meal forgotten, Timmy didn't protest as we headed down the concourse, following the signs to baggage claim. As Stuart had predicted, our bags were the only ones left. We presented our claim tickets, snagged our luggage (which, thankfully, included Timmy's Rolls Royce of a stroller), and schlepped our way toward customs.

"*Buona sera*," I said to the custom's officer, dredging up my little-used Italian.

"Name," he replied in perfect English.

"Kate Connor."

"Momma! Momma!" Inside the stroller, Timmy held his arms up for me. "I love you, Momma!"

My heart came close to melting. The officer looked unimpressed. "Occupation? Reason for visit?"

"Demon Hunter." Okay, I didn't say that. But I have to confess I was tempted. Instead, I reached down and scooped Timmy back up into my arms. "I'm a stay-at-home mom," I told the official as I caught Stuart's eye and smiled. "And we're here for the best vacation ever."

CHAPTER 2

One hour and fifteen minutes later, I was cursing Rome, city planners, and Henry Ford. If he hadn't shoved the automobile onto an unsuspecting public, then I wouldn't be sitting in bumper-to-bumper traffic on the *Via Aurelia* with a starving toddler, a cranky teenager, and a grumpy husband.

"Are we there yet?" Allie asked for the eighteenth time.

"Does this look like a B&B?" I snapped.

She glowered at me, flopped back in her seat, and pulled out her phone.

"No texting," I said. "You can send an email to Mindy when we get to the B&B, but texting is just too expensive. Besides, it's late in LA. I'm sure Mindy has things to do."

She let out an explosive breath, sagged further down into her seat, and pulled out her iPod. A minute later, she had her earbuds in and the music cranked up so loud I could almost make out the lyrics. I considered telling her to turn the sound down, but decided that teenage deafness was a small price to pay for a few moments of peace in the taxi.

Because my family does not travel light, we'd been forced to hire a taxi van. Stuart and Timmy were in the row in front of me, and my husband turned around now to face us. "So," he said with a grin. "*Are* we there yet?"

"Don't even start. How's Timmy?"

"Full up on Goldfish and fast asleep."

"That's something." I glanced out the window, trying to judge our location. I saw the sign announcing the exit for the A90, the highway that ran in a loop around the city proper, and sighed with relief. We weren't there yet, but once we were inside the loop it was fair to say we were making progress.

"Does it feel like home?"

I turned back to Stuart and found him watching me with a curious expression on his face.

"San Diablo traffic's nothing like this," I said, referring to our small California town. "Now, when I lived in Los Angeles—"

"No," Stuart said. "I mean Rome. How does it feel to be back?"

"Oh." I hesitated, searching Stuart's face for hidden meaning. He was talking about Rome, but was he really wondering about *Forza*? About my past with Eric, who'd also been a Hunter?

Eric is Allie's father and my first husband. He'd been my best friend, my partner throughout my early years as a Demon Hunter, and when we'd retired and moved to California, I'd looked forward to a long, happy, and normal suburban life. It hadn't worked out that way, and ten years into our marriage, Eric had been killed in a violent mugging—or so I'd thought.

I'd picked up the pieces of my life, met Stuart, fallen in love, and gotten married all over again. When Stuart and I had first started dating, he'd believed I was a widow with a nine-year-old daughter. True enough, but I'd neglected to tell him about my past. To be fair to me, I was retired at the time, and a history of killing demons isn't the kind of thing that comes up on your typical date. But I kept my mouth closed even after he put a ring on my finger. And even after we'd had a child.

Then a demon had crashed through our kitchen window and tried to kill me, and suddenly I was back in business. I still didn't tell Stuart, though. Not even after Allie learned my secret. Not even after Eric reappeared in my life, albeit in the body of another man, a scenario that, unfortunately, none of those marital help books even bother to address.

So much for typical suburbia, right?

In retrospect, I'd been a fool. I can now say with absolute authority that when your dead ex-husband mystically returns to life, it's always a good idea to let the current husband know. It's a trust thing, and I blew it. Stuart ended up learning about Eric's return at the same time he learned about my Demon Hunting past. And, no, it wasn't easy. Not on him, not on me, and not on our marriage.

And then, to make matters even more complicated, it turned out that the first husband I still loved—and who still loved me—had kept a few secrets of his own. Like, for example, the fact that a demon had taken up residence inside him.

Eric fought—hell, yeah, he'd fought. I'll even go so far as to say that he won. But there wasn't exactly a ticker tape parade in the streets of San Diablo after the battle. Horrified by what he'd done when the demon had taken control of his body, Eric had left San Diablo for Los Angeles, saying that he needed space to think.

And as for Stuart—well, it's one thing watching your wife fighting evil out there in the world. It's something else entirely when that evil is part of your extended family.

I'd like to say that I didn't blame Stuart for taking Timmy away—for fearing that the only way to keep my baby safe was to get him the hell away from me.

I'd like to say it, but I'd be lying.

Instead, I'd been heartbroken, furious, confused, guilty. You name it, I felt it. Allie and I had been alone, and I'd been lost in a red haze of emotion. Anger at Stuart for leaving and for taking Timmy. Guilt for wanting Timmy at my side, even though I knew that the very nature of what I was—what I did—meant that he would always be in danger. Anger at Eric for walking away. And, yes, guilt because I still wanted him there, despite the fact that I had another family. Another life.

I'd craved home and family, and it had been *Forza* I'd turned to. I needed the familiar comfort of the dorms—of the life that had once been the only thing I knew. And since Father Corletti had already suggested that Allie come over to train and study, the decision was an easy one.

Allie and I had been lost in a flurry of last minute preparations when Stuart and Timmy had arrived on the doorstep. He wanted to fight for me, Stuart had said. He wanted to fight for our marriage.

I believed him. So help me, I did. *I do.* And when I'd folded myself into his arms, it had felt as though I'd been blessed.

But my deep down, horrible secret? I didn't fully trust him—I couldn't, not after he'd left me. Not even though he came back. And no matter how close he held me—no matter how many times he apologized—that truth still hung there between us. Because despite "for better or for worse," he'd walked away from me, from Allie, from our family.

I'd made the decision to come back to Rome because I needed space to deal with that. To get my head around it.

And even though I meant every word when I said that I wanted this to be a kick-ass family vacation, I couldn't escape that tiny part of me that resented Stuart for coming along.

In other words, I was a mess. And the lack of sleep really wasn't helping.

"Kate?" Stuart was frowning at me now. "I didn't realize it was such a hard question."

"What? Oh! Sorry." I sat up straighter and managed a smile. "Sorry," I repeated. "Mind wandering. I'm tired. But yeah, it's good to be back." I glanced out the window again and saw that traffic had cleared and we'd made some serious progress. I hadn't recognized much of the area around the airport, but now that we were circling the southern edge of Vatican City and approaching the Tiber River, I was noticing familiar landmarks.

Places I'd walked with friends. Alleys I'd crept through on the hunt.

I caught a glimpse of the *Ponte Sant'Angelo* as we turned on to the *Piazza Pia*, and remembered the time that Eric and I had taken out a vampire that had interrupted one of our very first romantic strolls. I shot a quick glance at Stuart's face and decided not to mention that.

"That's the *Castel Sant'Angelo*," I said, pointing to the magnificent structure that had been commissioned by the Emperor Hadrian as a mausoleum for himself and his family. "I used to spend a lot of hours wandering those halls. It's a museum now," I added in response to Stuart's querying glance.

"We should go tomorrow," Stuart said. "Or even this afternoon. A quick nap and I'll be up for playing tourist."

"Sure," I said, even though what I meant was, "No." I wanted to go to *Forza*. I wanted—no, *needed*—to see Father Corletti. I wanted to give him a hug and hear his familiar voice. And I wanted him to brush his hand over my daughter's cheek and say, "Ah, *mia cara,* how much you have changed since last I saw you."

And wasn't that the truth?

Father Corletti had come to San Diablo after my first post-retirement adventure. He'd come to take personal charge of the Lazarus Bones, the ground-up remains of the bones of raised-from-the-dead Lazarus himself. Turns out that kind of thing is pretty important to demons, and a very nasty one had swept down on San Diablo hoping to do a little mischief. I'd managed to put a stop to it, and

Father had come personally to retrieve the sack of mystical dust and to welcome me back to active duty. What can I say? I'd gotten a taste for the excitement again. More than that, though, I understood exactly what I was fighting for. *My family.*

I glanced at Stuart and felt my heart twist a little. Truth was, I was *still* fighting for them. And so long as Stuart was trying, I would, too.

I drew in a breath and smiled. "Sure," I repeated as I reached forward to take his hand. "We'll do the museum whenever you want."

Beside me, Allie shifted. "*Now* are we there? Or at least close?" The van was maneuvering the narrow Roman streets, the driver frequently laying on his horn and swearing quite creatively in heavily accented Italian.

"Not far," I said. "If I'm remembering right, it's just a few more blocks."

"I think we could get there faster walking," Allie said, and I had to concede she had a point. Our plane had landed just after seven in the morning local time, and we'd come into the city during the morning rush hour. All things considered, it was amazing we'd arrived as quickly as we did.

"If you'd packed lighter, walking might have been an option," I teased. Though I'd begged, Allie had insisted on taking more or less everything she owned. I'd explained about the extra cost for overweight baggage. She'd countered that she was willing to pay it herself.

What can I say? I caved. So long as she lugged them and paid for them, she could bring all the bags she wanted.

"We can pile them all on Timmy's stroller," she said, then groaned loud and long. "I just want to *be* there."

"Me, too, kiddo," I said, thinking that her suggestion wasn't half-bad. The stroller was one of those massive contraptions that did pretty much everything for the active parent other than diaper the kid. It bent, folded, collapsed and maneuvered rocky trails. It boasted every possible amenity with the exception of a built-in DVD player, and I wouldn't be surprised if that showed up on the next model.

Despite all that, I didn't think that it could handle four suitcases, two carry-ons, a backpack and a purse. But I will admit I was tempted.

"*Borgo Pio?*" Our driver asked, then rattled off the street number.

"Yes!" Allie and I said at the same time.

Situated in a bustling shopping area, our bed and breakfast, the *Bonne Nuit*, was just a stone's throw from Vatican City. Not the *Forza* dorms, but close enough to visit.

"Mom, look!" Allie was pressed against the window pointing at something down the street. I shifted so that I had a view, and saw the dome of St. Peter's Basilica looming over us.

"St. Peter's," I said.

"Huh? Oh, yeah. I meant *that*. Look! That shop doesn't have anything but umbrellas!"

"Europe is a wild and wacky place," I said as my daughter rolled her eyes at me.

When the driver finally maneuvered the van in front of our B&B, I shifted from mom-mode to playing the role of a general directing the unloading of the van, a process I was well into when the heavy wooden door to the B&B opened and a beaming woman with a round face and an even rounder body emerged, her arms spread wide. "Kate Connor! And is Alison?" She glanced at Stuart, who held a drowsy Timmy in his arms. "And Stuart, no? And the bambino? He is Timothy?"

"Timmy," I said, stepping toward the woman. "You must be *Signora Micari*?"

"*Si! Si!* Come in, come in. My son, Paulo, he bring your things. Come," she beckoned when my family hesitated. "I show you room, yes?"

"Go on in," I said to Stuart and Allie. "I'll pay the driver." I wanted to wait for Paulo, too. As a Demon Hunter raised in the Church, my faith in God was strong. My faith in the gypsies and con artists who wandered the Roman streets? Not so much.

As it turned out, I was right to be leery. Because as I was counting out bills into our driver's eager palm, a skinny street urchin grabbed Allie's backpack off the pile and sprinted for a nearby alley. I smacked the last bill into the driver's hand and took off in pursuit. I didn't think I'd catch the kid. He was young and wiry, and considering the unkempt state of his hair and the grime-covered clothes, I assumed he was one of the many kids trained from birth to steal from the tourists. In other words, a pro who'd probably already dropped down into the sewers and was halfway to Milan by now.

I burst into the alley a few seconds after the kid did, certain I'd find nothing, and already rehearsing how I'd tell Allie that a good chunk of her belongings had decided to take off on a vacation of their own. Color me surprised when I found the kid waiting for me.

And even more surprised when his little fist shot out hard and fast, connecting with my jaw and sending me stumbling back against the hard stone wall of the alley.

CHAPTER 3

My head throbbed, and I could feel a lump rising from where it had connected hard with the wall of the ancient stone building. The kid—no, the *demon*—had his hands clenched tight around my neck. He was small, and he had to tilt his head back to look up at me. But his diminutive size didn't lessen his strength, and I was struggling to breathe as my vision narrowed, the periphery turning black as I gasped and choked in a futile attempt to suck in some much-needed oxygen.

"Where is it?" he asked, my mind barely registering that he spoke in perfect English. He lifted himself on his toes to get even more in my face. "*Where?*" he repeated.

I opened my mouth, struggling to make a sound.

He growled, then released his grip just enough so that I could answer.

I didn't bother. Instead, I thrust my knee up and pivoted my foot out, connecting hard with his shin. As I'd hoped, he was already off balance from raising himself onto his toes to get in my face. The good news was that he stumbled backward. The bad news was that his hands were still around my throat and he took me with him.

We tumbled to the ground, him on his back and me straddling him. I slammed the edge of one hand hard against his throat, and as he gasped, I drove my other fist straight into his wrist. He released my neck, and I sucked in bucketsful of glorious air— along with the rotten egg and vinegar stench of his nasty demon breath.

"Where is what?" I demanded, shifting my position so that my knee was hard in his groin and my finger was poised right over his eye, the kind of threat he couldn't ignore. That's the trouble with international travel—I didn't have anything sharp on me. I didn't even have a barrette, having pulled back my hair twenty-plus hours ago with an elastic band.

Which meant that if I wanted to end this demon, I was going to have to shove my finger into his eye socket. Gross, but it would have the effect of opening the portal that would suck the demon back into the ether.

The downside, of course, was that a sucked-out demon couldn't answer my questions. He'd be gone, and I'd be left beside a useless shell of a body. *Useless* being the operative term, because a dead demon couldn't tell me anything. And right then, I was jonesing for information.

Dammit, dammit, dammit! I'd known there were demons on the prowl, and yet I'd so desperately wanted a demon-free vacation that I'd called on toddler logic and pretended that if I just looked the other way it would all go bye-bye.

There was a lesson there. Something about never ignoring the sign of a demon, because if you did it would surely come back to bite you on the ass.

At the moment, my ass felt well and truly chewed.

I used my free hand to slam my fist soundly into his nose. "What?" I repeated. "What do you think I have?"

"You know," he snarled, and then he hocked back and spat on me. So help me, I flinched. Me, the woman who'd changed countless dirty diapers and nursed children through all forms of stomach flu. I faltered in the face of phlegm. And the demon took advantage of my weakness, wrenching his body to the side and forcing himself out of my grasp.

"Oh, no you don't," I said, grappling for him, but he was small and wiry and fast. He scuttled backward like a crab, then hopped to his feet.

"It will be ours," he said. "The door will be opened."

And then the little fiend turned and ran down the alley away from me. I started after him, but was halted by the sound of pounding feet behind me coupled with Stuart's worried voice, now echoing down the alley. "Kate? Oh, shit, Kate! What happened?"

He was at my side in seconds, holding my arm to steady me, then bending down to pick up Allie's backpack, which the little demon had dropped. At least I'd managed to accomplish that much.

"Are you okay?" He looked into my eyes. "Was it—"

"Gypsy," I said. "Snagged Allie's pack."

"Jesus, Kate. You should have just let him take it. What if he'd had a knife?"

"Force of habit," I said dryly. I rubbed the sore spot on my head as we walked back to the front of the B&B. "And all he had was a fist."

"So it wasn't a—a demon?" His voice dropped so far it was barely audible.

I shook my head, the lie coming too easily. "A kid," I said. I told myself it was just jet lag and hunger. I'd tell him the truth later, after we all were rested. But honestly? I think I was lying to myself, too.

"*Mom!*"

Allie's scream had me racing inside, terrified that the demon had doubled back to my daughter, and equally scared that I was going to get caught in my very own lie.

I found her on the B&B's narrow staircase, battling an unwieldy monster that was lurching down on her. "The brake!" I cried as I lunged forward, squeezing in beside her and taking the weight of the thing on my shoulder. "You need to set the brake! It can't roll back on you if you set the brake."

"Right. Sure. Got it." She dropped down onto her knees while I held the thing steady, then she reached under the carriage to set the brakes on the two back wheels of Timmy's monster-sized stroller.

Once the stroller was no longer trying to roll gleefully down the stairs, Allie squeezed in beside me and we maneuvered it back down to the lobby where Stuart waited with Timmy in his arms. In other words, exactly where the blasted thing had been trying to get all along.

"What were you trying to do?" Stuart asked.

She shrugged. "Paulo took the luggage upstairs. I was trying to help."

"Maybe we should ask Mrs. Micari if there's someplace we can store the thing downstairs. We don't actually need it in the rooms."

"Oh," Allie said. "Right."

"I'll take care of it," Stuart said, passing Timmy to his big sister. "Your mom's done enough this morning. I'll meet you in the room."

I hauled my exhausted body up the two flights of stairs, glanced around just long enough to recognize our luggage and confirm I was in the right place, and then collapsed face down onto the bed. I'm pretty sure I managed exactly ninety seconds of quality nap time before I was awakened by the pitter patter of tiny feet bouncing dangerously near my head.

I peeled my eyes open, rolled to my side, and watched as Tim made a game of plopping butt first on the bed, bouncing twice, then giggling like it was the funniest thing ever.

Maybe it was, but I was too wiped out to smile.

Stuart joined us in the room with the announcement that we were all set, and the stroller was tucked away in an alcove off the kitchen. "How's the bed?" he asked me.

I patted the spot beside me. "See for yourself."

He took me up on the invitation and lay back with a long, slow sigh. I knew exactly how he felt.

"This so totally sucks," Allie said. She was stretched out across the pillow-covered daybed that doubled as a sofa. "We just got here and you guys are already crashing. Hello? It's morning. It's Rome. We should be out. Doing stuff. Instead we're stuck in this tiny room. I bet the *Forza* dorms are like a hundred times bigger."

"Those rooms are even smaller," I said gently. I couldn't blame her for being disappointed. My original plan was to stay in the dorms and let her get a feel for where I grew up. More important, to let her see where her father and I met.

Once Stuart and Timmy had joined the excursion, I'd changed our plans, moving the family from the austere *Forza* dorms to the quaint little bed and breakfast that Father Corletti's secretary had recommended.

"Sorry," Allie said, but there was no apology in her voice. She shot a glance at her little brother. "But at least let the squirt sleep with you because if he wets the bed, I am *so* not going to be happy."

Before I could respond, there was a sharp tap on the doorframe. Stuart hadn't closed the door, and when I turned I saw Mrs. Micari standing in the doorway, her sparkling eyes focused on Allie. "You like the rooms, yes?"

My daughter's brow furrowed. "Rooms?"

I caught Stuart's eyes and saw my own grin reflected there. I considered chiming in to deliver the good news to Allie but decided to let Mrs. Micari take the role of fairy godmother.

"But of course. Is good for children to have their own space, yes?" She turned slightly and winked at me. "And good for the adults, too. For the *amore*."

"Ew!" Allie said, but I could tell that the horror of contemplating *amore* between Stuart and me was completely overshadowed by the fabulous reality of her own room. Albeit one she had to share with her baby brother.

She turned imploring eyes on Mrs. Micari. "You're serious? Timmy and I really get our very own room?" She didn't wait for the innkeeper to nod. In one giant leap, she moved from her perch on the day bed to the mattress where Stuart and I had moved to sitting positions. Her arms went around me, knocking me backwards before releasing me and turning the same attention to Stuart. "Thank you, thank you!"

She turned back to Mrs. Micari. "This is the best hotel ever!"

Mrs. Micari's grin widened. "In that case, it is not necessary for me to give you this?" She indicated the basket she held in her hand. "Is biscotti and fruit. And also," she added with a sideways glance toward me, "the *Torta Barozzi*."

"Seriously?" I'd started to rise from the bed. *Torta Barozzi* wasn't a traditional Roman dessert, but I absolutely love it, not in small part because it provides a massive hit of both chocolate and espresso, two of the major food groups.

Allie got to her feet before I did and took the basket from Mrs. Micari's outstretched hand. "Best. Hotel. Ever," she repeated.

"Bed and breakfast," I corrected, but she waved off my words.

"Can I see it? Can I see my room?"

"That you share," I clarified.

"Yeah, yeah," Allie said. "You know he's gonna want to sleep with you guys."

I considered arguing. After all, *wanting* and *getting* were two different things. And I fully intended to delve into that whole *amore* thing that Mrs. Micari had so expertly advocated. But time enough for that later. Right now I was just pleased to have a daughter who'd sloughed off her initial disappointment and was giddy about the accommodations.

Mrs. Micari smiled wide and stepped out into the hallway. Stuart and I followed. The B&B had five rooms, two on the first floor and three on the second. Our rooms were on the second (a fact that confused Allie since, in Italy, the first floor is the ground floor, the second floor is the first, and the third is the second). The room Stuart and I shared was on the left side of the landing, next to the huge, modernized bathroom. Allie and Timmy's room was the first of the two rooms on the right. The third room had been let to a young woman who, according to Mrs. Micari, was traveling Europe with a backpack and a train pass.

The kids' room had two beds, a recliner, and a small television, which attracted Timmy like a magnet. "*Blue's Clues,* Momma? *Blue's Clues?*"

"Not here, kiddo."

"There's probably something for him," Stuart said, flipping it on. "Disney's international, right?"

Mrs. Micari laughed. "You speak Italiano? Is no English on television channels here."

"Seriously?" Considering her tone, Allie might as well have cursed out loud.

"Allie." Hopefully from *my* tone she could tell that she was walking a fine line.

She shot me an apologetic smile then glanced at Mrs. Micari. "It's no big. We're so totally not going to be watching television. And if the kid gets bored, we've got movies for him on the iPad."

As she spoke, she took the remote from Stuart and randomly hit the channel button. Commercial. Commercial. Italian soap opera. Commercial. *I Love Lucy* (dubbed). News. Commercial.

News.

My mind caught up with the image. "Allie," I ordered, interrupting Mrs. Micari's rundown of the room's amenities—fresh towels, bottled water, treats every evening. "Go back."

My daughter shrugged and complied. A second later, she and I were both staring at a televised scene from a familiar airport concourse—right in front of the men's room.

A reporter was speaking in rapid-fire Italian as paramedics and armed *polizia* moved in and out of the facility. "—found dead, although authorities have released no additional information other than the man's identity," the reporter said in Italian.

Allie looked at me, waiting for me to translate. I was just about to do that when the reporter continued speaking. "The victim has been identified as Los Angeles resident Thomas Duvall, a passenger on TransAtlantic flight 832."

"Which TransAtlantic flight?" Stuart asked as the image on the screen changed, the view of the concourse replaced by a single passport photo.

I didn't answer. For that matter, I'd barely heard the question. All my attention was on the screen—and the larger-than-life image of Mr. Pepperdine looking back at me.

CHAPTER 4

I stared at the television, absolutely certain that if I could get my hands on the incident report, I'd see that Mr. Pepperdine—aka Thomas Duvall—and his stinky breath had been taken out by a ballpoint pen to the eye. Or something equally pointy.

Because there was no other way to kill a corporeal demon.

Actually, that's not true. Beheading also tends to remove demons from bodies, but only because the demon doesn't want to hang around anymore. The whole point of hiding inside the human form is to blend in with the general populace. Without a head, that whole blending-in plan doesn't work out too well, and the demon voluntarily vacates its human home. Stick a pencil through the eye, and there's nothing voluntary about the departure. The portal opens and—*poof*—the demon's sucked back to the ether, swirling all around us without form, biding its time until it can try again with another dead body.

"Wasn't he on our plane?" Stuart had edged closer to the television, and though he glanced at me, his attention was mostly focused on Allie. Apparently I wasn't the only one who had noticed the way she'd spent much of the flight staring at a demon in a cute guy costume.

"Yeah," Allie admitted. "He sat a few rows up from us."

"Good God," Stuart said, leaning in to turn up the sound, which made no sense at all, as Stuart doesn't speak a word of Italian. "We were in that concourse." His worried glance fell on me. "You were probably in the ladies' room when that guy was killed."

A few feet away, Allie gasped. "Mom, you didn't—"

I twisted to face her, my expression dark with warning.

"—see anything?" she concluded lamely. "When you went to the bathroom, I mean. You were right there. Did you see something?"

"No," I said firmly, because Stuart obviously hadn't gone there yet, and Mrs. Micari was still standing in the doorway. And what was she thinking, anyway? That I'd take out a demon in the middle of the airport in Rome? Italian security officers patrol the airport with machine guns, and somehow I don't think they'd believe me if I said I was saving the world. "I didn't see a thing."

A big fat lie, of course. I'd seen more than I cared to think about, actually. I'd seen Duvall catch sight of a maintenance man and then turn the other direction. And I'd seen another maintenance man guarding the door to the men's room in order to, I now assumed, keep unsuspecting travelers away from the sight of the dead demon sprawled out on the shiny Italian tile. Were the maintenance men with *Forza*? Rogue demon hunters? Unsuspecting civilians?

I didn't know and, frankly, I hoped I wouldn't have to find out. After all, *Forza* headquarters was just a ten minute walk from here. Even if something was up—and, really, where demons are concerned, when is something *not* up?—that didn't mean I'd end up knee deep in it.

Did it?

"Poor bastard," Stuart said. "I hope they catch who did this."

"I hope they find out why," I said.

"Is for the police," Mrs. Micari said. "Is no way to start a vacation. You forget about this, yes? Rest now. Nap. And when you wake I will make you lunch and you explore the city. *Si?*"

"That sounds like heaven," I said.

"Seriously?" Allie countered. "You're really tired?"

"Yes," Stuart said, and Allie rolled her eyes in apparent astonishment at how completely lame adults were when it came to traveling.

"Relax," I said. "Enjoy having a room all to yourself." She snorted. "A room without adult supervision," I corrected.

"Elmo!" Timmy shouted. He'd picked up the remote and had started flipping channels. Sure enough, Italian Elmo was there on the screen. Timmy couldn't understand a word, but considering he'd probably memorized every episode of *Sesame Street*, I don't think it mattered.

"Oh, great," Allie said.

"That's why God invented the iPod. Two hours," I promised. "Then we'll go explore."

The truth was that I had more than enough energy to go with her right then. But there were other things I needed to deal with first.

Stuart and I left the kids in their room, and once we reached ours he tugged me down to the bed beside him. "A room all to ourselves," he said. "Too bad I'm too exhausted to enjoy it."

"I won't consider it a mark against your manliness," I promised. "And the room will still be here tonight."

"Set an alarm?" His eyes were drooping, already half on his way to sleep.

"I'll take care of it." I sat up. "I'm going to find the bathroom. Back in a sec."

In a sec, I had a feeling he'd be out cold.

I didn't actually need the bathroom, but I did want out of the room, and that seemed like as good a place to make a phone call as any. When I got there, though, I found the door locked. I tapped. "Allie?"

I didn't get an answer, but I thought I heard a short sob, followed by the splash of water.

"*Allie?*" I repeated, my mommy senses in overdrive.

"No." The word was low and harsh, but the voice was definitely teenage. I remembered what *Signora* Micari had said about our floormate—a teenage girl doing the backpacking around Europe thing. I pictured Allie just a few years older than she was now traveling by herself with nothing but some cash, a train pass and her iPod, and my heart twisted a little for the girl.

"Are you okay? Can I get you anything?"

Silence, and then the distinct sound of a nose being very soundly blown. "I'm okay," she said. "Sorry to hog the bathroom. I'm—I'm going to be a few more minutes. Okay?"

I hesitated, wanting to help but at the same time knowing it wasn't my place. I didn't know this girl. Didn't know if she was missing her family or if she'd just had a fight with her boyfriend. For that matter, maybe she'd just spent the last two hours watching *Sleepless in Seattle* on her iPod and all she wanted was a good cry. Bottom line, I had problems of my own.

"My name's Kate," I said before I walked away. "If you need anything, I'm in the room at the top of the stairs."

Not that I was going right back to my room, but I didn't expect that the girl would come calling any time soon. And if she did? Well, Stuart had lived with a teenage girl in the house for years now. I figured he could handle the drama.

I found an ornate powder room on the ground floor just off the foyer. I went in, turned on the water, sat down on the closed toilet, and pulled out my phone, intending to make one of those extremely expensive international calls to my best friend, Laura. Despite the fact that demon hunting was supposed to be one big huge secret, Laura had known about my extracurricular activities almost from the moment I got sucked out of retirement. At the time, I needed to either tell her or let her believe she was going stark-raving mad. What can

I say? I considered it my duty save my friend's sanity. And, yeah, I was keen to have a confidante.

Since then, pretty much the entire population of San Diablo had learned my secret (okay, not really, but sometimes it felt that way), but Laura was still the first one I turned to when I needed help with the hunting of demons, the commiserating about marital problems, or the creation of truly delicious baked goods. What can I say? The woman was a goddess in the kitchen. Me? Not so much.

Today, demons were on the agenda. Pepperdine University was in Los Angeles, just a short drive from San Diablo. I was hoping Laura could get on the Internet and find out when Thomas Duvall—the real Thomas Duvall—had died. Because the poor kid *had* died—and not in a Roman restroom. No, he'd died back in the States, and as soon as he had, a demon had moved in.

That's how most demons take human form. Sure, there are other ways, but possessing a body is messy, and time-sharing with a human means you have to find a human who's either so evil or so power-hungry that they're willing to give up some free will to let a demon's essence move into the body with them. Fortunately for the world at large, there aren't too many people like that.

No, most demons are opportunistic. When a person dies, their soul leaves their body, and for a short window of time, a portal is open allowing the demon—who was previously wandering around in the ether all noncorporeal and frustrated—to slide inside, just as pretty as you please. Usually it's the victim of a heart attack, a drowning, a violent car crash. The kind of situation where EMS is certain they've lost the guy, but then to everyone's surprise he draws a sharp breath and the flatline jumps into a nice, steady pulse. The newspapers often call those incidents miracles. The newspapers are wrong.

Fortunately, demons can't just hop into any dead body. If they could, we'd be surrounded by corporeal demons. (The truth is, we *are* surrounded by noncorporeal demons. They're out there in the ether, all around us, all the time. Kind of creepy when you think about it. I try not to. I figure until they've got a solid form they can't bother me. And once they are solid, I know what to do about it: kill them.)

No, demons have to find just the right body. It has to be newly dead, and the demon has to slide in before the portal closes. Even then, it's not necessarily a sure thing. Some bodies reject a demon. I'm no theologian, but the way I understand it, the souls of the faithful hang around, protecting the mortal shell until it's safe from infestation. In other words, the faithful fight.

Thomas Duvall, I assumed, hadn't put up much of a struggle. He'd dropped dead, and a demon had dropped in.

What I wanted to know was why.

Most demons slide into humans simply because that's what they want—*humanity*. Sure, they want to traipse around stirring up trouble, but they want to be flesh while they do it. They want the sensations. The emotion. The highs and the lows. But that doesn't usually include international travel. If a demon wants to be flesh in Italy, it makes a lot more sense to slide into an Italian body.

But Duvall went from Los Angeles to Rome. Why? And was it coincidence that he was on the same plane as a Demon Hunter who had recently defeated some of the most powerful demons in the world? (Not to seem immodest, but I'm talking about me.) Had he been on some kind of vendetta? And if so, why not just take me out in the airport? Why play nice and return my son's bear?

And if Duvall had been planning to take me out, then who stepped in to protect me?

I didn't know, but I wanted to find out. And I figured that starting with the man himself was the best place to begin. Especially since I had no other starting point.

I pulled out my phone, then realized I'd forgotten to turn the thing back on after we got off the plane. I pressed the button and waited for the signal bars to show up, irritated when I realized I'd missed a voicemail. Probably Laura calling to make sure we arrived safely.

But the call wasn't from Laura. It was from Eric.

"It's me," he said, his voice sounding far away and hollow. "I know I may be the last person you want to hear from, but I thought you needed to know." My chest tightened as he continued. "I just found out that the cathedral's altar was destroyed a few months ago. Apparently the bishop kept it quiet because he didn't want the press descending, but someone leaked it and there was an article in the paper this week. Seems the bishop had a replacement brought in, and with the cloth covering it, no one was the wiser."

He cleared his throat. "Anyway, I called Delores as soon as I read the article," he said, referring to the cathedral's volunteer coordinator, a woman who had her hand in all the church's business. "She said they don't have any idea who the culprit was or why anyone would desecrate the altar."

I shivered, disturbed. The altar in San Diablo was infused with the bones of saints, as was the mortar of the cathedral itself. In theory, that kept demons away, although San Diablo had more than its fair share of the beasties lately. Humans, though, could come and go as they pleased. And humans often did the bidding of demons, stealing holy relics for use in black magic rituals.

Maybe it was just random mayhem, but I doubted it. Some demon was up to something, and I didn't have a clue as to what.

On the line, Eric continued. "Listen, maybe this could have waited until you got back. But the truth is, I've got a bad feeling. Don't trust anyone. I know you're half a world away, but watch your back, okay? And for God's sake, keep an eye on Allie. I—I couldn't stand it if anything happened to either one of you."

The words were simple and straightforward, but they weren't what I heard. Instead, I heard, "I love you," and my eyes brimmed with tears. This was the Eric of my past—a man I loved, the father to my oldest child.

"Dammit," I muttered, then shoved the phone in my pocket. I forced thoughts of Eric-the-ex-husband from my mind and concentrated on the words of Eric-the-Demon-Hunter. He'd always had a sixth sense about danger. Couple that with the fact that Mr. Pepperdine had schlepped from California to Rome, and I had to believe that my gut instinct was right. Something bad was brewing, and I didn't have a clue what it was.

I hit the speed dial button for Laura and tapped my finger on the side of the toilet as the phone rang and rang, finally dropping into voicemail. "Hey," I said. "It's me. I just realized it's after midnight, so you're probably asleep, but I could use your help. Not a crisis," I said, hoping that was the truth. "But call me as soon as you get this. Okay?"

I ended the call, frustrated because I doubted I'd hear from her for at least six or seven hours. I considered calling Eric—I'd never known him to go to sleep before 2 a.m.—but I wasn't yet strong enough to make that call. His voice I could handle. A full-blown conversation? Not yet. And certainly not on one tiny catnap.

I am nothing, however, if not motivated, and I left the bathroom determined to do my own research. And, yes, cursing the fact that I still hadn't taken Laura's advice and bought an iPhone when I'd given in to the demands and bought one for Allie as a pre-trip treat. Now I was going to have to get the laptop out of Allie's room. More important, I was either going to have to lie about what I was doing or tell my daughter the whole sorry truth.

I was saved from deciding which route to go by Mrs. Micari. She was sweeping the foyer when I stepped out of the powder room, and her face lit up when she saw me. "You do not sleep?"

"Restroom," I said. "The one on our floor was occupied."

"My young guest," the woman said. "She is a good girl, I think. Not much older than your Allie."

"And she's traveling by herself?"

Mrs. Micari shrugged, as if to say *these kids today*. I didn't question further. Maybe the young woman was a prodigy. Maybe she and Allie could hang out and the other girl would be a good influence on my easily distracted daughter. Who, I had to admit, did a damn good job when she put her mind to it. I just wanted to see her excelling at her actual schoolwork. Not at the researching of demon lore.

"You are hungry? Thirsty? You do not sleep, but perhaps you would like the coffee?"

"I'd like coffee very much, thank you."

What was probably once a morning room right off the foyer now served as a dining area. Light flooded in through a wall of windows that overlooked an herb-filled back garden with a small statue of the Virgin Mary. In the garden, two cushioned outdoor chairs sat on either side of a small tiled table. An elderly man slept in one of the chairs, a newspaper folded in his lap. "Your husband?" I asked.

"No, no. That is *Signor* Tagelli." She offered no further information and, since it really wasn't my business, I didn't pry. "Sit," she said, indicating a small table near the door with a white table cloth and a bowl of fruit on display. "You like the cream? The sugar?"

"Just cream," I said. Usually I drank my coffee black—demon hunting only burned so many calories, you know—but I was on vacation. Time to go a little wild and crazy.

She bustled out through a set of swinging doors at the far end of the room, and I took the opportunity to take a look around. I liked what I saw. The place was warm and inviting. Knickknacks, flowers, and small framed photographs filled dozens of shelves, and yet the room didn't look cluttered. There was no dust. No collections of knick-knacks. Either Mrs. Micari was a far better housekeeper than I was, or business was good enough that she could hire help. The second was better for my ego, but it was the first that I believed.

"Coffee and biscotti," Mrs. Micari said, returning to the room with a wooden tray laden with a small coffeepot and a large basket of the delicious Italian cookies. She slid the tray onto the table, took a mug from the nearby sideboard, and poured me a cup. I added cream, then used the biscotti to stir my coffee. I took a bite of the coffee-drenched treat, closed my eyes and sighed. St. Peter's might be just around the corner, but I'd found heaven right there.

I opened my eyes to find Mrs. Micari smiling down at me, and I realized a second too late for good manners that I should have invited her to join me. I covered my mouth so I wouldn't spew her with crumbs and waved at the other chair.

She sat, hands folded in front of her primly on the table.

"Please," I said. "Share."

"No, no," she said. "I do not want coffee. I wish to speak to you."

"Oh. Sure." Without thinking, I reached for the travel pouch I still wore around my neck and under my T-shirt. Had we underpaid the deposit? Did I need to find someplace else to store Timmy's stroller? Had Timmy already broken something? "Um, what's up?"

She drew in a breath. "Katherine," Mrs. Micari began, and I stiffened. No one called me Katherine. No one except Father Corletti, the head of *Forza Scura*. "You must be careful," she continued as the little hairs on the back of my neck tingled a warning. "The city can be dangerous. For tourists. And for—for others as well."

"Others?" I said. I hesitated, then decided I had to take the plunge. "What kind of others?"

"Your kind."

"And what kind is that?"

The slightest of smiles tugged at the corner of her mouth, and I felt a cold chill run through me. "The kind that wouldn't be shocked to learn that the young man at the airport was killed by a stiletto through the eye."

CHAPTER 5

I shoved back my chair. "Who are you?"

"Ah, my child, the years truly are unkind. Have I changed so much?"

I stared at her, confused. I didn't know that face. And yet—and yet there was something familiar about her. My chest tightened, but this time not with fear but with the bittersweet tug of memory. "*Signorina Leone?*"

Her smile burst wide across her face, her eyes crinkling at the corners. "*Si.* Although it has been *Signora Micari* for many years."

"But I don't understand. You run a bed and breakfast? Why didn't Father Corletti tell me?"

Signorina Leone had been on the periphery of *Forza.* A maid, really. She'd done our laundry, cleaned our floors, helped make our meals. I'd never known her that well—she'd been quiet and observant but never involved in our teaching or our missions. But she'd always been there, and it was a bit like a miracle that she was here now.

"My husband Leonardo and I open this place after I retire. He has gone to God now, and I continue the work without him. Father Corletti, he is one of my best referrers."

"Does he—I mean, do you mostly let your rooms to Hunters? Or other people from *Forza?*" I thought about the teenager sharing our floor, not to mention the anonymous guests with rooms below us.

Mrs. Micari laughed. "No, no. Most of my guests find me through the Internet." She reached for my hand and squeezed it. "Is one reason I am so happy to see you. You are like a gift from the past, no?"

I squeezed back. "I know exactly what you mean."

I clutched her hand a bit longer than I probably should and was surprised to find that my eyes had filled with tears. I'd barely known this woman, and yet the thought that I was truly back—that I was really here, in Rome, connecting with my past— completely overwhelmed me.

When I finally released her, I found her beaming at me.

"But tell me now of the man that you married," she said. "I see young Eric's eyes on the face of your daughter. But your youngest—his father was not raised within *Forza.*"

"No."

"And yet he knows the truth."

"Some of it," I said, realizing only as I spoke that it was true—I still hadn't told Stuart everything. Oh, he knew the basics. But the battles in my youth? The demons who still held vendettas against me? The violent, fear-based passion of my early years with Eric? Those weren't stories that Stuart had heard.

"And our dead Mr. Duvall? Your husband knows the truth about that?"

"*I* don't even know the truth," I said. "I don't have any real proof he was a demon. And even if he was, I'm here on vacation. Thomas Duvall may have been on my plane, but that doesn't mean he's my problem." I said it in my firmest voice—the one I use to tell Allie she's not allowed to wear makeup. But I wasn't fooling myself. Unfortunately, I don't think I was fooling Mrs. Micari either.

"No?"

"This is Rome, *Signora.* I'm a stone's throw from at least a dozen Hunters, trainees and adepts. I came here for a vacation. Not a fight." *That* much at least was true. I was afraid, however, that a fight had found me.

Mrs. Micari's mouth twitched. "Katherine, child, it is true that I was little more than a servant when you were young. But that does not mean that I am a fool."

"I—"

"Tell me honestly—did danger follow you here from San Diablo? Was that boy a demon? More important, was it you who killed him?"

And there it was. Flat out. Specific. A question that I could either answer or not. But I couldn't avoid it with vague words and ambiguous responses.

Twenty years ago, I wouldn't have even considered hedging. She might not have been a trainer, but she was part of *Forza*, and that meant that I'd trusted her absolutely.

But things had changed.

I couldn't tell her. Not that Duvall was a demon. Not that I hadn't killed him. Not even that I had my suspicions about the demon-y status of the airport's maintenance crew.

Eric said don't trust anyone. And as much as it sucked, "anyone" included Mrs. Micari.

I smiled at her and managed a casual little shrug, hoping she couldn't see that it was tainted by guilt and regret. "I really don't know if he was a demon." Technically true, but it still felt like a lie. "He was on our plane. He was an attractive young man. And now he's dead. Beyond that, I don't know anything. And," I added, increasing my lie exponentially, "I don't see how he could have anything at all to do with me."

"Don't you?" An odd smile twisted her mouth. "Have your instincts become so dull, or is there perhaps another reason that holds your tongue?" I heard the hurt in her voice, and I almost gave in. *Almost.* But didn't. Not because I had the strength, but because I caught a glimpse of a familiar figure easing across the foyer and realized I had an excuse.

"Allie!" I called. "Why aren't you watching your brother?"

She appeared in the doorway immediately, her expression contrite. Too contrite, frankly, and I wondered what she'd overheard. "I'm sorry! I'm sorry! He's sound asleep—I swear—and I really needed to pee." Her mouth snapped closed even as her eyes widened with mortification. "I mean the bathroom. I needed to use the bathroom and there was someone in the one on our floor and so I came down here to look for another one and then I heard you guys and—" She ended with a deep shoulder shrug. "I shoulda said something, I know. But—well, anyway. I still need a bathroom, so. . . ?" She trailed off, eyes on Mrs. Micari, who pointed helpfully toward the powder room.

Allie started sprinting that direction so quickly that I didn't doubt the story about needing the bathroom. Too bad. I needed her to be my excuse.

"Hold up there, kid," I said as I rose and started across the room. "I'm sure the bathroom upstairs is free by now. I'll go up with you." I flashed a smile toward Mrs. Micari that I hoped translated as, *kids—whatcha gonna do?* "We need to have a little chat anyway . . . "

"Oh." She bounced slightly from one foot to the other. "Um, okay. See you later, Mrs. Micari."

"*Si,*" responded the woman who was more than just our innkeeper. "Katherine," she added, the lilt in her voice and slight nod making my name sound like a promise rather than a dismissal.

I followed Allie up and waited on her bed until she returned from the bathroom. "So, on a scale of one to ten," she began, "how much trouble am I in?"

"For the snooping? Five. I'm cutting you a break since it was an unplanned snoop." I looked pointedly at her brother, whom I'd found asleep underneath a bedspread in front of the television. "For babysitting duty, I'm going with negative three. What if he'd pulled over furniture instead of just a blanket?"

"I wasn't planning on being gone that long. Honest. And it's not like he actually got hurt. I mean look at him," she added, pointing to the bed where I'd carried him just a few moments before. "Conked out like a little angel." She smiled wide, revealing two rows of sparkling, newly brushed teeth.

I sighed, relenting. The kid was alive; the lecture could wait.

Allie must have picked up on some subtle shift in the temperature of my mood because she plonked down on the bed next to me. "So, a five? Seriously? 'Cause I can totally live with a five."

With effort, I managed not to laugh. "You didn't set out to snoop, so you get credit for that. But mostly you're coasting on the fact that I wanted an excuse to avoid Mrs. Micari's questions."

"In other words, snoop again and I'm in trouble."

"I have such a smart daughter." I pushed myself up. "Nap. Or listen to music," I added before she could protest that she wasn't the least bit tired. "We'll go play tourist as soon as Timmy's up and Stuart's ready to go."

"But Mom—"

"Don't 'But Mom' me."

"—did you kill it? The Thomas Duvall demon. Was that you?"

"Did you see the security guys walking with the automatic weapons? Do you think I'd be happy in an Italian jail?"

"Well, sure, I get that. But—it's just—I mean, he *was* a demon, right?"

"I think so," I admitted, sitting back down again.

"And he's dead." She left the sentence hanging, dangling like bait on a hook. I didn't nibble. After a moment, she let out an exasperated breath. "If you didn't kill him, then who did? And what was a demon doing on our flight? I mean, that's weird, right?"

"They have to get around somehow," I said dryly. In truth, I was proud of her. She was asking all the right questions, and she deserved to know as much as I did—even though I knew exactly squat.

Except I didn't want to tell her. Not about the altar. Not about the call from her dad. My heart might be bursting with pride from how capable and grown-up my daughter was becoming, but that didn't mean I wasn't still completely twisted up inside. Grappling with her desire to step into this life. And grappling with my willingness to let her do it. Weren't parents supposed to protect their kids? The skills she was developing made her stronger, sure, but they also meant that danger would come her way. More, it meant that she'd seek it out.

And, dammit, this wasn't the place I wanted her doing that. I wanted this trip to be about family—not about the family business.

But that was just me making excuses. There was danger out there whether she sought it out or not. It was there whether she trained or not. For better or for worse, this life was in her blood, and I owed my almost-adult daughter the respect of telling her what I knew. And what I suspected.

She sat stiff and silent beside me on the bed, scowling and undoubtedly certain that I was going to blow her off.

Once again, I stood. "Come on." I bent down and carefully scooped Timmy into my arms. He stirred but didn't wake, and I said a silent thank you to the patron saint of overwhelmed mommies.

"Where?" Allie asked. "Are we getting Stuart?" I heard both wariness and defiance in her voice. If I said yes, my daughter was going to put up a fight.

"No," I said. "We're leaving Timmy with his dad. Then you and I are going to take a walk. We'll leave Stuart a note telling him we decided to get a head start on shopping."

"But we're really. . .?"

"Shopping may be involved," I admitted. "Mostly we're going to talk." I was even considering heading to *Forza* so that I could run through everything with Father Corletti before bringing Stuart by to take the official tour.

And yes, I felt guilty about that. Probably not as guilty as I should. Lies and secrets were becoming second nature to me. Not a good thing, but there you go.

Allie's grin lit up her eyes. "I want some shirts and jeans, but mostly I want a jacket. Italy's all about the leather. Oh, and I told Mindy I'd find a purse for her. Something really exceptional, you know?"

I didn't bother answering, just moved slowly out the door with my bundle of toddler in my arms and my teenager in my wake. Two minutes ago, she'd been all about the demons and the mysteries. Now it was shopping and fashion and soft leather accessories.

I could only imagine what the next minutes would bring.

CHAPTER 6

Timmy is the type who wakes from a nap if you breathe too loudly, but he stayed asleep in my arms all the way to the other bedroom. Just one more benefit of international travel: intense toddler exhaustion.

Stuart lay sprawled across the still-made bed, his arm draped over his eyes and his chest rising and falling with his steady breath. Allie danced impatiently in the doorway as I tiptoed to the bed and gently put Timmy next to his father. I stood there frozen for a moment, not daring to move. One beat. Then two. Then three.

I drew in a relieved breath, then moved slowly and carefully to the window to quietly close the drapes. A ribbon of light moved over the bed, slowly growing thinner until it brushed the top of Stuart's head, then slipped away into the gray light. Stuart didn't move. I didn't breathe. Another beat, then I tiptoed to the tiny desk and scrawled a note on the provided stationery.

Allie can't sleep. T's out like a rock. Doing the girlie thing and getting a head start on shopping. Text me. XXOO

I propped it up against the phone and headed toward Allie, giddy with success. My fingers closed around the doorknob, and I tugged gently.

Didn't matter. The inevitable *squeeeeeeeek* filled the room. I swallowed, eyes fixed on Timmy, who remained blissfully, beautifully still.

Stuart, however, sat up.

He blinked groggily. "Kate?"

"Hey," I whispered. "Go back to sleep. Timmy's zonked and you look like you could use another hour or two."

His head lolled to one side as he glanced at Tim. "If you're sure you don't mind."

"Trust me. This way's much better for our marriage. Less communal shopping is a good thing."

"For the good of our marriage, then," he said as I bit back a smile of pure victory. "Go."

That victory, however, was sadly short-lived. Because the moment Stuart flopped back on the mattress, Timmy lurched up. He thrust his arms out and a cry of "Mommy, Mommy, Mommy" sprang from his lips.

I rushed to scoop him up, catching a glimpse of Allie's head making dramatic contact with the doorjamb. I wasn't unsympathetic, but I also couldn't abandon my little guy.

"Okay, okay. I'm up, too." Stuart punctuated his words by getting out of bed and stretching. "For the best anyway, I guess. Don't all the travel books say you should avoid napping? Better to slug it out and then go to bed at a reasonable hour. Gets you over the jet lag faster."

"Adults, maybe. But cranky toddlers? Maybe we should try to put him down again? Allie and I can come back in an hour. Even a little nap could make all the difference."

Stuart eyed me. "You'd rather we stay behind?"

"No, no. Of course not." I was glad he was up. I was glad Timmy had wakened. This was *Rome*, and I loved this city, and I wanted to share every square inch of it with my family. *I did.*

And yet . . .

And yet I didn't. Because "every square inch" would mean *Forza*. All of *Forza*. Not just the tour, but the truth—what I needed to know. What I needed to learn.

"Every square inch" meant bringing Stuart into the loop. Maybe I hadn't realized there was even going to be a loop when we boarded the plane in California, but I knew it now. And I knew I wasn't ready to tell him. I knew from the way my mouth got dry and my stomach clenched and the words seemed to die on my tongue. I *needed* to share with my husband; any marriage counselor in the world would tell me that sharing is the path to healing.

Needed to. But didn't want to. Because I didn't trust him. Not fully. Not yet.

It broke my heart to admit it, but I couldn't run from the truth any more than I could ignore a rampaging demon.

I'd have to tell him the truth soon—I got that. But soon wasn't now. And so Allie and I waited with varying levels of impatience as Stuart and Timmy got ready. All things considered, they didn't take too long, and we were down the stairs in less than fifteen minutes, ready to do some serious sightseeing and shopping. I knew this because Stuart had his earmarked copy of *Frommer's Guide to Rome* under his arm. "You may know the city," he'd said to me on the plane as he highlighted section after section. "But I want to make sure we don't miss something exceptional." Apparently Stuart had as much faith in my skill as a tour guide as he had in my cooking.

"Go get the stroller," Stuart said to Allie when we reached the foyer.

I held a hand up to stop her. "That thing is a leviathan," I said. "Do we really have to take it?"

"He'll last three minutes walking, and I won't last much longer than that carrying him."

"I have an idea," I said, then went in search of Mrs. Micari. Three minutes later we were armed with directions to the Roman version of *Babies "R" Us*, just a little over a block away, right across from an ornate and ritzy hotel I'd been inside only once. A Syrian diplomat had died in the penthouse apartment, and a demon had taken advantage of the opportunity. Eric and I had climbed the fire escape to the roof, shimmied down some old piping to the balcony, broken in, and taken care of that little problem.

It had been my most James Bondian mission.

And I have to say that it's one heck of a nice hotel.

We lucked out and found a cheap umbrella stroller in a sale bucket right in the front of the store. Within half an hour we were back on the street and heading toward the *Via Cola*, one of my absolute favorite places in the *Borgo Pio*. "We don't have to do the shopping thing now," Stuart said. "I know you're anxious to see Father Corletti. Why don't we go to *Forza* first?"

From behind Stuart, Allie's eyes went wide. I looked down, focusing on pushing the stroller on the uneven street without injuring my son, myself, or an unsuspecting pedestrian.

"No can do," I said, once again displaying my amazing skill at the deceitful arts. "I called while you were napping. He's booked solid until later. And this works out great. Allie wants to shop, and we all need to eat." And, now that I thought more about it, the longer I put off seeing Father, the more likely I would have heard from Laura about Thomas Duvall. Always nice when your manipulation and deception actually serves a legitimate purpose.

We turned the corner and paused, taking in the site of the white stone marketplace and the quaint shops covered by a smattering of flowering vines. *Home.* It hit me right in the gut, and I reached out automatically for Stuart's hand. It was right there, and he held me tight, twining his fingers in mine.

"I never even came here that often," I admitted. "But it's just—"

"You've missed it."

"Yeah," I said. I raised myself up on my toes and kissed him. Truth was, I missed more than just Rome. "I love you, you know."

He met my eyes and held them a beat longer than I expected. "I know," he said. "I love you, too."

"Guys," Allie said. "Seriously? This is a vacation, not a honeymoon. Two kids with you, remember? Can we get on to the good stuff?"

I laughed. "And that would be?"

"Duh. The clothes. I mean, look. There. *Right there*." She was pointing to a leather goods store two doors down, and I knew immediately what had drawn her attention—a very stealthy looking black jacket hanging limply on a too-skinny mannequin in the store window. "Can we?"

I considered. "Tell you what. Tim and I will head to the market and get some things for lunch," I said, referring to the Trionfale market. "There are tables over there, see? Meet me there in half an hour and we'll eat."

"Better idea," Stuart said. "I'll endure the trauma of clothes shopping while you get the food, and then we'll take a picnic lunch to the Trevi fountain."

"Oh, can we, Mom?" Allie asked.

I consulted a mental map. The subway station wasn't far. And we *had* bought a stroller for easy traveling. And Stuart had spent all those hours highlighting his guide book. . .

"Sure," I said. "Thirty minutes? Right here?" We'd paused by an ornate fountain.

"Roger," Stuart said and saluted.

I rolled my eyes. "Watch your wallets," I admonished, looking at both of them in turn. "From pickpockets and," I added, focusing on Stuart, "from overeager teenagers who will undoubtedly fall in love with the first jacket they see."

"I hear Rome is overflowing with that type," he said, then waved me off. Allie was at the shop door before I'd even gotten Timmy's stroller turned around.

"Okay, kid. It's you and me."

"I hungry," he said, then shoved Boo Bear's ear into his mouth and bit down. I frowned. Not because the bear was filthy and my child was in danger of contracting impetigo (whatever the heck that was) or some other dread disease. But because I knew better than to let the bear leave a hotel room. But it was too late now. We were just going to have to be extra, extra careful.

One close call with a stuffed friend was one too many, and I doubted that if we lost the bear again that there'd be another nice friendly demon around to help us.

The market really was amazing—filled to the brim with booths and stations selling every manner of cheese, meats, fruits, vegetables, breads, pasta, coffee and on and on and on. I made a mental note to bring Allie and Stuart back, especially in light of Allie's newly implemented all-natural, all-the-time eating regimen, which I expected to last at least until she found a package of Italian cookies too tantalizing to pass up.

I bought a couple of pounds of sliced salami from the butcher's stand and some bread from the baker next door. The fruit stand was at the end of the hall and I maneuvered that direction, cursing the stroller, which really wasn't fair since it was actually Timmy's age and corresponding little baby legs that were the problem. Despite how many people lived in Rome—and considering how many of them either had children or were once children themselves—it is not a city conducive to maneuvering with kids.

This was not a Fun Fact that I remembered from my days living here.

We made it without banging into any unsuspecting pedestrian's shins, running over any toes, losing Boo Bear, or encountering a pickpocket. We hadn't even bought any fruits and vegetables, and already I considered the venture a success.

I grabbed a flat-bottom totebag lined with linen. It had a rather pathetic drawing of St. Peter's printed on one side and an image of the Italian flag on the other. It cost fifteen American dollars and I'd be surprised if it lasted the week.

I didn't even hesitate. I plunked my bread and sausages into the tote, hooked it over my shoulder, and started to inspect the fruit, trying to decide what everyone would eat. A white-haired woman in a green apron peered at me through narrowed, pinprick eyes. Considering the stroller, I couldn't believe she thought I was going to bolt, but I reassured her just in case, enjoying another chance to speak my rusty Italian.

Not even three words were out of my mouth when her dour expression shifted, her eyes widened, and her face took on a warm, friendly vibe. I didn't bother telling her that today I was a tourist. We'd bonded, she and I, and I listened as she reviewed in painstaking detail the quality and flavor of each of her wares. "Try," she said in Italian, slicing off part of a fig and holding the juicy morsel out to me. "And for your little one, too."

Timmy wasn't strapped into this stroller, and he was on his feet and reaching for the fruit in seconds. The woman beamed, and as I watched her smiling at my son—my precious little almost-three-year-old—I saw just a flash of a girl on the other side of the stand. *Allie?*

For a second fear clutched me, but then the crowd shifted and I saw the girl again. Not Allie. This girl's hair was blonde and shorter. But the shape of her face was so similar. And those eyes— her eyes were so like Allie's it was uncanny.

Without thinking, I took a step toward her, which was absurd because not only did I not know that girl, but there was a huge display of melons in front of me. I didn't touch the fruit—I'm certain I didn't even come close—but suddenly I was caught in an avalanche of melons. The entire display seemed to be tumbling to the ground, and Timmy was standing there, hands flailing, suddenly squalling, and trying desperately to turn around and run away from the fruitapalooza.

"Tim!" I reached for him, but he went down too fast, slipping on a splattered melon. I bent to help him, but another pair of arms scooped him up first.

Time does a funny thing when you're terrified, and I was scared to death in that moment. I saw right away that the arms belonged to a woman, but I didn't know her, and my thoughts ranged from kidnapping to demons to black magic rituals involving innocent children. A mother's fears surrounding her children were vivid enough—

throw my particular profession into the mix and scary didn't even begin to describe it.

"Give me my son," I said, slowly and calmly in crisp, clear Italian. I didn't have a weapon handy— I *knew* I should have unpacked the suitcases before we went out—but I grabbed a carrot off the produce stand. In a pinch, it would do.

The woman looked at me as if I were insane. "He fell," she said in English. She smiled brightly at me, her brown eyes shining, and then at the once again dour produce seller who was currently shouting and tossing her hands about behind us, complaining loudly to no one in particular about how we had ruined her. *Ruined* her.

I knew I hadn't started the melee. But I had my fears that Timmy had somehow been involved.

"Did you see what happened?" I asked the woman as she put Timmy down and he toddled to me. I scooped him up and held him in my arms.

She nodded, her dark curls bouncing as she urged me closer, her eyes on the produce lady. I expected her to tell me that Timmy had pulled out a single piece from the bottom. The keystone fruit upon which all the other fruits depended.

What I didn't expect was the hand on my shoulder as she faced me and leaned in close, or the press of a knife to Timmy's soft neck as she sandwiched his body between us. The icy chill of fear shot through me, and I tightened my grip on the carrot and forced myself not to move. Not to do anything that might upset her.

"Protect it," she whispered, leaning even closer so her mouth was near my ear.

"Get the knife away from him, or I swear I will end you."

"You'll do nothing to me while your child is at risk," she said, her voice so low I could barely hear it over Timmy's whimpers. "But it is not me who is your enemy. I am nothing. Protect it with your life, because if the lock is opened, there will be no lives left to protect."

With astonishing swiftness, she shifted the knife, moving it from Timmy's neck to mine. We locked eyes, and I caught the minty scent of too much mouthwash. Then she turned, darted into the crowd, and was gone.

I dropped the carrot and clutched my son even tighter against my chest. In my arms, Timmy was still crying. Not because of the danger—I doubt he even knew there'd been a danger—but because of the noise and the crowd and the fact that everything was just too damn much.

I counted to five, allowing myself only that brief time to be horrified. Then I kissed his head and shifted him to my hip. As I did, I saw the produce lady looking at me, her brow knit in concern. I didn't know if she'd seen the knife. But I knew she could tell I was scared.

Behind her, I saw the girl again. The one who looked like Allie. She stood on the far side of the produce stand, a stack of cantaloupe piled in front of her. She was staring right at me, not with the baffled expression of a shocked witness, but with the understanding countenance of someone who knew exactly what was going on.

Allie. Stuart.

I clasped Timmy tight and bolted toward the exit, then stopped and doubled back. I'd forgotten the umbrella stroller.

I had no idea if demons had attacked Stuart and Allie, too. But I did know my husband. If they'd been ambushed, Stuart was going to be pissed, but he'd probably forgive an abandoned stroller. But if I left the stroller behind and all was well?

How the heck was I supposed to explain that?

"Mom!" **Allie squealed** the second I burst through the doors of the boutique. But it wasn't terror that put that high pitch in her voice. It was lust.

Not for a boy. Not even for a dessert.

This was clothes lust.

She twisted and turned in front of a trifold mirror, trying to see the jacket from all angles. "Isn't it awesome? And it's just like yours." She thrust out her arm to reveal a cuff that looked like it hung loose, but had a hidden interior cuff that clung to her wrist. The idea was to block the weather. I used it as part of a mechanism I'd hooked up for delivering a spring-loaded stiletto.

Stuart quirked a brow. "Practical clothing for the fashionable dem—"

"Go to Daddy," I said quickly, releasing a squirming Timmy and giving his bottom a farewell pat.

"Sorry," Stuart said, his glance darting quickly to the slender woman sorting inventory behind the nearby counter. "I am the very epitome of discretion."

"So can I get it?" Allie asked. As far as I could tell, she'd been completely oblivious to my conversation with Stuart who, I noticed, hadn't scooped up Timmy. Instead, he was fondling a finely crafted briefcase while our son plonked down on the floor and started digging through baskets filled with leather wallets.

I cleared my throat to get his attention and then looked pointedly at our busy little boy. Stuart shrugged guiltily, then retrieved the kid, who howled in protest and made a move to eat a billfold. I quelled my maternal urges and looked away, hoping that Stuart could wrangle the wallet free before we had to buy it.

"Mom!" Allie thrust her arms out, demanding my attention. "Hello? Can we get it?"

"How much?"

She shimmied out of it and started searching for a price tag which, naturally, she didn't find. I asked the sales girl who, as far as I could tell, had decided we were nothing more than annoying tourists, and it was in her best interest to ignore us. Even my Italian didn't loosen her up.

"Four hundred and twenty-five American dollars," I told Allie, trying to not reveal my sticker shock to the girl while at the same time communicating to Allie that there was no way in hell she was getting that jacket.

"So can I get it?"

Apparently my communication skills left a lot to be desired.

"We'll think about it," I said. "Come on. It's already past noon."

"What's for lunch?" Stuart asked as Allie sighed and moaned and made a show of returning the jacket to the rack.

I reached for the tote bag with the sausage and bread, then realized that I must have lost it at the market. "Ah, right. Well, I thought we'd go to this fabulous little café I remember near the Spanish Steps," I said, leading my troops out the door. "Assuming it's still there."

"I thought we were picnicking."

"That was my first plan," I said brightly. "But the lines at the market were insane. And then I remembered the café and thought that would be a fabulous place to have our first Roman lunch. Besides, they have an amazing wine list. Or they did. Okay?"

"Sure," Stuart said agreeably. Allie, however, was peering at me with much more comprehension.

What happened? she mouthed.

I looked pointedly at Stuart, who was occupied with coaxing Tim back into the stroller. *Later*, I mouthed back.

Stuart didn't notice our exchange, as he was already running down the itinerary he'd planned while I'd been in the market. "We can have lunch first, of course, but if we're already in the area, I'd like to do as much as we can. The Spanish Steps, the Trevi Fountain. Maybe even the Colosseum and the Forum. What do you think?"

I thought it sounded like way too much for a family that included a toddler, but I kept that opinion to myself. The truth was, I wanted away from the *Borgo Pio*. I wanted to get lost in a crowd.

I was feeling exposed—and that wasn't a feeling I liked.

Not that there weren't demons in all those places Stuart listed. In fact, there were probably more. You might think that the looming presence of St. Peter's basilica would keep the nasties away, but you'd be wrong.

As a general rule, demons avoided places with a lot of holy relics and holy ground, but there were exceptions, and Rome was high on that list. Because while demons couldn't walk on holy ground—not without a whole lot of pain—they'd endure the torment if there was something they really wanted. And Rome had a lot of stuff that demons wanted. Relics, icons, mystical doo-dads. Holy, yes. But black magic rituals usually required something sacred. And demons were all about the black magic. Which meant that Rome was the big leagues, and any self-respecting demon wanting to pull off something major was going to make a pilgrimage sooner or later.

To be fair, it wasn't all about the snatching of holy items and the desecration of sacred places. It was also about being close to the enemy. If the Church was training Demon Hunters, well, it only made sense for the demons to hang around and try to learn as much as they could about our elite little force.

Those, at least, were the commonly accepted explanations for Rome's rather hefty demon population. Personally, I thought the real reason was something deeper. I hadn't delved too far into the psychology of demons, but I'd been around long enough to pick up on some truisms. And the

biggie? Demons wanted what they couldn't have—
they wanted to experience humanity. What's more
human than faith? We could go our whole lives
without ever truly knowing that something greater
waits for us beyond the curtain of death, and yet we
still believed. We still had *faith*.

I couldn't remember a time when I didn't know
that there were unseen things that shared the world
with us. Dark and scary things that lived in the
ether and sought a toe-hold on this life. I knew
because I saw. And because I'd seen the darkness,
my faith in the light was strong, and I'd clung to it
with desperate determination.

But I'd often wondered if my faith would have
been so strong if I'd lived a different life. If I'd
been another Kate growing up in the Midwest,
going to church, playing on a farm. If I'd never
seen a real demon and my fears about what might
be hiding in the closet never came true. I liked to
think that I would believe just the same, but I
didn't know if that that was true. And whenever I
met a person with true, deep faith, I knew that I'd
encountered the heart of what made us all truly
human.

"Kate?" Stuart thrust his arm out, stopping me
before I walked into traffic. "Where are you?"

"Sorry. I was just—memories. It's great to be
back, but a little weird, too."

"I'm glad we came. I want to share this with
you. Timmy, too, even though he won't remember
the trip."

"No," I laughed. "He won't. Allie refuses to
believe that she ever had a crush on Captain Hook.
But then I whip out those pictures from when she

was three, and suddenly I have a whole cache of prom night bribery photos. It's awesome."

"Pictures!" Allie blurted from behind us. "I forgot my camera!"

"I thought that was one of the reasons we bought you an iPhone," I said. "It has a camera built in."

"Mo-*om*. Hello? Rome. I want the real camera. I want to be able to zoom and do effects and all that stuff. I mean, I schlepped it all the way here and I promised Daddy I'd take a bunch of awesome photos, so. . ."

She trailed off, and I sucked in a breath. Her father had bought her the camera—a fancy Nikon—as a present for the trip that, I was certain, was also supposed to assuage his guilt for leaving San Diablo. I wasn't sure how his guilt was doing, but I did know that Allie loved the camera.

"Fine," I said because what else could I say? I pointed down the street to the subway station. "We'll meet you guys right there," I said. "We should be back in less than ten minutes."

"So?" Allie said as we hurried back to the B&B. "You haven't changed your mind about telling me, right?"

"I haven't," I said, then brought her up to date.

"But what is 'it'?" she asked. "A key, right? Because she mentioned a lock?"

"That's what I'm thinking."

"So it was probably stolen from the cathedral, don't you think?"

I *did* think, actually, and I was impressed that my daughter made the jump. "What makes you think so?"

"Duvall was on the plane," she said. "I mean, he came from California all the way here, right?"

"So you think Duvall had our mystery key?"

"I dunno. What I really think is that he assumed *you* had it. Like that's why he was on the plane. To follow you."

"You might be right." I glanced at my watch. Not yet one. "Laura's probably still asleep, but once she checks out Duvall's background, maybe we'll know more."

"What's that going to tell us? I mean, by the time we saw him, he was already a demon. Does it really matter what his body was doing before that?"

She had a point, but I didn't want to admit it. That's me, the eternal optimist. Fortunately, I was saved from answering by the fact that we'd arrived back at the B&B. "Where's your camera?"

"In my backpack."

"You gave it to Stuart on the plane so he could switch out the batteries."

"And he gave it back."

I handed her the key to the room Stuart and I shared. "Just in case I'm right."

She rolled her eyes, but didn't argue as she sprinted for the stairs. I watched her go, tapped my foot, then glanced at my watch. Stuart and Timmy were perfectly safe (I told myself) but I still wanted to hurry back to them.

"Katherine?"

I jumped, then turned to find Mrs. Micari behind me, her hands hidden under a dishtowel.

"You are back so soon." Her gaze darted from me to the stairs and then back to me again. "Is something wrong?"

"Not a thing. Allie just forgot her camera."

"Ah, I see." Her lips pulled into a thin line.

"Is that a problem?"

She waved my words away as if they were the silliest thing she'd ever heard. "Is nothing. The cleaning. I have just waxed the bathroom floors." Her tone was casual and the tight lines of her face disappeared so completely that I had to wonder if I'd imagined them.

"Signora," I began, but that's as far as I got before I was interrupted by the high, powerful punch of Allie's scream.

And this time, I knew it wasn't about a jacket.

CHAPTER 7

I took the stairs three at a time and found Allie standing in the middle of my ransacked room. Every single piece of luggage had been opened. Every single item of clothing had been tossed out. Drawers hung open and empty. The mattress lay askew, most of its bulk now held up by the floor.

I didn't say anything. I didn't even curse. Because what the hell was there to say?

"I don't think they even took anything," Allie whispered. She thrust her hand toward me and I saw the camera, the brand new Nikon that Eric had bought for her. Definitely not the kind of thing your average thief would pass up.

"It was on the floor, just right there on the floor," Allie said. "Like they couldn't care less."

I was certain she was right—demons weren't big on scrapbooking, and they rarely have Facebook pages.

From behind us, Mrs. Micari drew in a sharp breath. I whipped around to face her. "What the hell did you do?"

Her hand flew to her chest. "Katherine, no!"

But I wasn't interested in hearing it. I pushed past her into the hall and sprinted to the bathroom. As she'd said, the floor was damp, the entire room smelling of disinfectant. Proof she was innocent? Or proof she knew how to manage a cover-up?

Allie's footsteps pounded down the hall, and she came to a breathless stop behind me. "Mom, it wasn't—I mean, there was someone in the room when I got there."

I went cold. "What?"

"The window," she said. "It was open and he ran out. A kid. Grungy. I didn't get a good look, but I bet he was—"

"A gypsy. Right." What she really meant was 'a demon,' but since I hadn't told Mrs. Micari that I'd actually made the acquaintance of any local demons, I wasn't going to say so out loud. Allie's eyes darted to our innkeeper and back to me.

"Looking for stuff to sell, probably," Allie said. "And I guess I came in before he loaded the good stuff up."

"Looks that way." I turned to our hostess. "*Signora*, I'm sorry. I—"

She waved her hands, shooing away my words. "No, no. You are right. Is my home, is my responsibility. I do not understand, though, how this child got in." She frowned, then turned back toward our room.

I followed, then hesitated, taking Allie's hand and tugging her to a stop. "Your room?"

"It's fine," she said. "I opened the door, remembered you were right, and turned around to go to your room. But I saw it. Nothing messed up at all. Well," she added with a shrug, "not more than normal, anyway."

Mrs. Micari stood at the window in our room, peering out. There was no balcony, no fire escape. Just a decorative iron railing below the window on which potted plants could rest. Somehow the acrobatic little imp had managed to balance on the rail, get our window open, and get inside.

How he managed to scale three stories to get up in the first place I had no idea.

I opened the window wider and poked my head out, wondering if there was piping on the wall. Nothing. Just two more similar pot rails—one for the bathroom and one for the next guest room.

"Maybe he's just really good at climbing," Allie said. "The wall's pretty rough. I know some guys at school who could manage it." She gnawed on her lower lip. "I shoulda run after him. If I'd just looked out the window, maybe I could've seen which way he'd gone."

"And maybe he would have attacked you and maybe you'd be injured right now. You did fine."

"Is true," Mrs. Micari said gently. "The best fights are those you walk away from. And the even better fights are the ones you do not have at all."

"I guess," Allie said, but she didn't sound convinced. I hid a grin. Allie, I'm sure, was running an alternate history in her head. One in which she'd arrived in time to not only catch the demon, but to beat a confession out of him. Me, I was fine with the reality in which she was safe and unscathed.

"Will you stay here with Allie?" I asked Mrs. Micari. "I should go get Stuart and Timmy. They're waiting at the subway station."

"What?" Allie asked. "You're going to *tell* Stuart?"

"Sweetheart, yes. The possibility that Duvall was a demon is one thing. We don't even know for sure." I looked at her hard as I said that, trying to silently communicate that Mrs. Micari was not in my Absolute Truth loop. Not yet. "But if someone is breaking into our room, then Stuart needs to know."

"Mom. . . " She sank down onto the edge of the bed, looking more miserable than I'd seen her in ages.

I glanced helplessly at Mrs. Micari, who brushed my arm in a gesture of support. "You talk. I go now. But I clean up if you wish. Your husband, he does not need to know of this. Not until you are ready to tell him."

And there it was, that wave of guilt. She was being wonderful and supportive, and I was clutching secrets to my heart.

"Thank you," I said, hoping she could tell from my voice how much I meant it.

She closed the door gently behind her, and I went to sit beside my daughter. "He needs to know," I said.

"But it's demons. No matter what you said about gypsies, we both know he was a demon, right?"

"Pretty sure," I said.

"Well, what if he leaves again?" she asked, her voice so small I could barely hear it. "Daddy's already gone away. What if Stuart goes again, too?"

"Oh, baby." I put my arms around her and pulled her close. She put her head against my shoulder and clung to me, as small and fragile as a child. And she was still a child. Growing up, yes, and too damn fast. But still a child.

"Please, Mom. Please don't tell him. I—I don't want Stuart and Timmy to go away again."

She pulled back and looked at me, her nose red and her eyes bloodshot. She blinked, and a single tear trickled down her cheek. I brushed it away with the side of my thumb. "Okay," I said, hoping I wasn't risking my marriage while protecting my kid. "We'll have our perfect tourist day, we'll talk with Father Corletti, and then we'll decide what to tell Stuart. Fair enough?"

She snuffled and nodded even as I silently wondered if maybe I could wrangle a way to send Stuart and Timmy safely back to San Diablo. Then again, "safely" and "San Diablo" didn't necessarily go together anymore.

I was stuck between the proverbial rock and the hard place, and the only way I could get free was by figuring out what the demons wanted. What *it* was.

I had a mission. I just didn't have a plan.

CHAPTER 8

Considering how eventful the day had been so far, it was both a surprise and a relief when we were able to travel across Rome by subway without incident. Or, I should say, without demonic incident. The subway was crowded and Stuart edged too close to a non-demonic (presumably) street urchin who had his sticky little fingers on Stuart's money pouch before I noticed and slapped his hands away.

The kid glared at me, shoved his way toward the front of the car, and proceeded to try the same scam on a ruddy-faced man in a New York Yankees baseball cap.

"Holy crap," Stuart said after we'd shouted a warning at our fellow tourist. "Persistent, aren't they?"

"And damn good at what they do." Fighting was one thing—beat someone up, take their wallet. Tried and true and very risky. But sidling up to someone and sneaking off with their belongings without your victim even being the wiser? There was a certain elegance to it. Not that I wanted to shake the kid's hand and congratulate him on perfecting his trade, but that didn't mean I couldn't admire the skill.

"Between this and that gypsy in the alley, we're really soaking in the local color," Stuart said cheerfully.

"Color?" Allie repeated.

"Think of it this way—you'll be telling the gypsy-on-the-subway story for years. You can't buy those kind of memories in the local street market."

As Allie rolled her eyes, I looked at my husband with affection, then pulled him in close for a hug. "Thanks," I said. "And you're right. Even so," I added, aiming a stern eye at both him and Allie. "Be careful. The last thing we need is to spend the day at the Embassy because someone's passport got nipped."

We spent the rest of the ride guarding our belongings and watching each other's backs. I'd gotten used to constant vigil, but I could tell that such an extreme level of self-awareness exhausted Stuart, and by the time the train pulled into our final destination near the Spanish Steps, he'd lost a bit of that traveler's shine.

The doors swished open and Allie practically dove out, with me calling for her to wait right there on the platform as I helped Stuart maneuver Timmy's stroller.

"God, Mom, I'm not six. You don't have to remind me of every little thing."

"I know," I said. "But I've grown pretty fond of you over the last fifteen years. I really don't want to lose you in a crowd."

She rolled her eyes yet again then rattled off a sentence in choppy Italian.

"What did she say?" Stuart asked.

"I'm lost and staying at the *Bonne Nuit* bed and breakfast on the *Borgio Pio*. Please, can you help me get back there?" Allie recited.

"You taught her that?" Stuart asked me, making me feel all the more guilty for not thinking about teaching any of them even the most basic Italian.

"Hello? Technology," she said, holding up her shiny new iPhone. "I totally downloaded an app. I can say all sorts of stuff now."

What can I say? The kid had impressed me.

We'd gotten off the train at the Spagna stop on Metro Line A, and after wrestling with Timmy's stroller, we'd ascended to street level between the *Villa Borghese* and the *Villa Medici*, one of my favorite museums.

Stuart immediately unfolded a tourist map he'd grabbed from a display back at the B&B. "Okay." He turned in a circle to get his bearings. "Trevi Fountain, that way," he said with a kind of fierce determination in his voice.

"We're doing the Spanish Steps, right?" Allie asked. "I mean, hello? Pictures. And lunch, right?"

"Right," I said. "And we don't even need to rush to get to the fountain. There's a wonderful park nearby. And it's not like there aren't fountains here at the *Piazza di Spagna* and the *Piazza Trinita dei Monti*," I added, referring to the piazza closest to us, as well as the one we would reach once we'd climbed the steps.

Allie rolled her eyes. "A park?"

"The *Villa Borghese* Gardens," I said. "It's huge. With all sorts of stuff like children's rides and a lake and boat rentals. Actually, we could skip the café I was thinking of and find lunch in the park." I didn't mention that Eric and I used to rent the row boats during our rare free time, and that the park played front and center in my favorite memories of my early days in Rome.

"A park," Allie repeated, then swept her arm out to encompass the crowded, bustling, ancient city center. "Hello? History. Rome. Architecture. *Shopping*. I mean, come on. Seriously?"

"We've been on a plane all day," I said. "We're exhausted. And Timmy may look calm right now, but I can promise you that crankiness is imminent. He needs to burn off some steam."

"Yeah, but—I say again—*a park*?"

I looked to Stuart for help and didn't find it there. Instead he shrugged sheepishly and waved the map. "Not really on my list," he said. "But the Trevi Fountain? Kate, we're talking *La Dolce Vita, Roman Holiday*."

"There was that scene in *The Lizzie McGuire Movie*," Allie added helpfully.

"And *Gidget Goes to Rome*," Stuart added, this time waving not the map but one of the pocket-size tourist books he'd bought back in San Diablo.

I'd been in enough battles to know when I was defeated. "Fine," I said. "We'll get some pictures of everyone on the Spanish Steps, then we'll head that direction."

"Can we eat first?" Allie said. "Because I'm really hungry, and I need to use the bathroom."

"That's the plan," I said. It's not like I could argue, especially since my demon-in-the-market encounter had left us without a picnic lunch. I glanced around, trying to get my bearings. "I was thinking of this wonderful little café right in the *Piazza de Spagna*," I said, pointing vaguely in the right direction. I aimed a wry grin toward Stuart. "And it has a fountain."

"I'll throw a few coins in, but you're not deterring me." He held up the book. "I am Tourist. Hear me roar."

Allie groaned—the kind of sound that suggests her parents are just too embarrassing for words and started walking toward the *Via di San Sebastianello* in the direction I'd pointed.

I took the stroller from Stuart, grateful that Timmy had nodded off with Boo Bear still clutched tight in his hands. As with most of the roads in Rome's ancient center, this one wasn't smooth, and the lightweight umbrella stroller bounced and skipped. With each jolt I held my breath, fearing rampant crankiness if Tim awoke early from his nap.

The poor little guy must have been completely conked out, though, because he'd been thoroughly shaken by the time we'd followed the road around to the actual piazza, and hadn't even stirred.

"Wow," Allie said. We were facing south, the length of the piazza spread out in front of us, and two small grassy islands dominated the view. Allie dropped to one knee, the camera aimed at the cluster of palm trees. "It's like we're back home in

California," she said. "Except, you know, for the really old buildings and all the people speaking Italian."

"Except," I said with a smile.

Beside me, Stuart took my hand. "It's lovely here."

"This used to be one of my favorite places. When we weren't totally jammed up we'd come here and walk the perimeter and look at all the shops then go sit on the Steps and soak up the sun."

"Just looking at the buildings is enough for me," he said, turning to take in the ancient buildings that rose around us in a variety of colors, from muted ochre to vibrant rose.

I followed his gaze, trying to look at this place through his eyes. I'd grown up here and back then it had simply been home. Now, though, the beauty truly stood out. The majesty of the buildings. The subtle distinctions of texture and style. The age and honor of this thriving city that for so long had been the focal point of not just the Church but the whole world.

I'd been a piece of it, and that had felt wonderful.

Now I lived in a house of plywood and siding and laminate, with a heart that came not from the age or the beauty or the majesty of the architecture, but from the family that lived inside. My family. And that felt wonderful, too.

I squeezed Stuart's hand, my earlier doubts vanishing with a wave of contentment. I nodded toward Allie, then at Timmy. "Thanks for coming with us."

He bent to kiss my head. "I couldn't be anyplace else."

I let go of his hand so that I could slide my arm around his waist. "Want to get to work on your tourist checklist?"

"You know me so well."

"Spanish Steps." I pointed vaguely ahead of us and to the left. "You can't really see them from here, but that's why all those people are hovering just past that tea shop. Come on," I said, then started walking. "Steps, Allie. Let's go get you your pictures."

"Still *really* need the bathroom," Allie said.

"Why don't we eat first?" my ever-reasonable husband suggested. "Then we can see the Steps and do some shopping here on the piazza," he added with a significant look toward my very pleased teenager.

"And after that, we'll do the Trevi Fountain," I said as I led the way diagonally across the square to Gusto, a family run restaurant that I was pleased to see was still thriving.

"We can hold off on that," Stuart said gently as we paused outside the restaurant. "There's still the visit to *Forza* this afternoon.*"

"Oh," I said, still not wanting to take the entire family, and wishing that I had the guts to just say that outright. "Right. But I—"

"I'll take Tim back to the B&B while you and Allie go," he added, his warm eyes full of understanding. "I know you want some time with Father Corletti alone." He glanced toward Allie. "Well, you and our girl."

My throat clogged with tears. "Thank you."

"You don't have to thank me. I get that he was like a father. Which is why I still want to meet him. But I understand. Really."

I nodded, feeling more centered than I had since we'd landed in Rome.

The hostess arrived and led us to a table outside, right at the edge of the seating area so that we had a front row view from which to soak up the touristy goodness.

"This is wonderful," I told the waitress in Italian, then asked her where the bathroom was. She pointed around the side of the building, and Allie bolted. I ordered her a Coke, a juice for Timmy, and then a bottle of red wine for me and Stuart.

"Living dangerously," he said. "As exhausted as we both are, you may end up back at the B&B with me, sound asleep on the bed."

I reached across the table and squeezed his hand. "I can live with that."

In the stroller, Timmy stretched, then yawned, then blinked his eyes open. I saw the beginnings of crankiness on his face, and quickly retrieved a Ziplock bag of Goldfish crackers from the front pocket of the diaper bag.

That seemed to do the trick, and after a sleepy mumble that I interpreted as "Thank you," he started to shove fistfuls of the fishies into his mouth.

Since the piazza is a high tourist zone, I expected the menu to be in both English and Italian, but apparently the family that owned it was all about tradition because Stuart tossed the menu at me and said simply, "I'll just go with pasta and see what shows up."

I did a quick skim of the menu, then glanced back up at him. "Do you trust me on lunch?"

"That depends. Are you cooking or ordering?"

I narrowed my eyes. "Watch it, Connor."

He laughed. "I trust you completely to order," he said, and so when the waitress came back with our drinks, I did just that, ordering practically everything on the menu because I was feeling both hungry and decadent.

Since I felt covered by a layer of subway grime, I pushed back from the table and left Stuart in charge of the munchkin. I followed Allie's path, circling the building until I found the dingy metal door that led into Gusto's storage area. I found the sign for the ladies' room well inside the building, past shelving stuffed with bags of flour and baskets of vegetables.

I expected the door to be locked, but when I pushed inside I found a nicely remodeled restroom with three stalls and even a small bench where customers and the overworked staff could sit and take a load off.

I grabbed one of the paper towels, dampened it, and started mopping the city grime off my face. "Don't just go for pasta," I said to Allie. "Try something new, okay?"

I expected an answer, and when one didn't come, I frowned, then peered down to look under the doors of all three stalls. No feet.

Panic stabbed me right between the ribs, but I told myself that it was okay. That she was back at the table with Stuart and Timmy. True, I hadn't seen her in the alley or as I'd rounded the building, but knowing Allie she'd decided to cut through the kitchen, annoying the owners and the chefs and the waitstaff.

Despite that soothing mantra, my panic didn't lessen, and I burst out of the restroom and into the storeroom again. I almost turned toward the kitchen, but figured if she was in there, she was at least safe. My real fear was that she'd stepped out into the alley, gotten sucked up by the wilds of Rome, and I'd never see my daughter again.

I am nothing if not paranoid, especially where my kids are concerned. And considering what I knew about what hides in dark corners, I couldn't help but think my paranoia was justified.

I was through the exit in less than five seconds, and I paused there, looking around for evidence of a struggle. But all looked well and I told myself that I was overreacting. That if I just went back to the table, she'd be there chowing down on bread and soda and rolling her eyes when I delivered yet another lecture on being careful.

I told myself that, but I wasn't convinced. Still, even if Allie wasn't beside me and wasn't at the table, that didn't mean the worst. She was fifteen. Odds were good I'd find her in a nearby boutique. She'd end up grounded for life, but I could live with that.

But when I pulled out my phone to text her, I didn't even have time to call up her number when I heard the sharp, clear cry of "*Mom*" from behind me.

I backtracked, racing farther into the alley, past Gusto's back door and into a narrow passage filled with wooden fruit crates, broken-down cardboard boxes, and one wiry old man with sun-worn skin and a huge knife pressed against my daughter's throat.

I froze, my mind spinning through my options. To be honest, there weren't many. Any move I made could set him off, and even from several feet away I could tell that the knife was sharp. One quick flick of his wrist, and my daughter was dead.

Allie had to know that as well, and yet she stood perfectly still and looked completely composed. Yes, there was terror in her eyes. But behind that I could see determination and calculation. And in that brief shock of the moment I was struck hard by the brutal truth that I'd been doing my best to ignore—this life was Allie's calling as much as it was mine.

"What do you want?" I asked, my voice low and even and my eyes on Allie's.

"Hand it over or the little bitch dies," he said in perfect English.

In that moment, I would have handed over pretty much anything, from my wallet to the key to hell. Too bad I didn't have a clue what he was talking about.

"Do it!" he shouted.

I held my hands up, surrender style. "Okay," I said. "Okay. I just have to get it." I made a show of reaching into my purse. "Just give me a second."

I might not know what he wanted, but I did know that when Allie and I had gone back for the camera, I'd shoved my favorite knife into my purse, the same one that I'd been spending time throwing in the backyard with Allie. My skill throwing a blade was probably better than it had been in fifteen years, but that didn't mean that I was thrilled about throwing it in the general direction of my daughter's head.

Her eyes had gone wide, and I hoped to hell that she could read my mind.

"Let her go," I said. "Then I'll toss it to you."

"Do you think I'm a fool?"

I hoped he was, but I didn't answer.

"Give it to me now, and the girl lives."

I didn't believe him, of course. Even if I had the thing, he would cut Allie. Not only because demons were just that way, but because he had to know that I would run after him—but not if my daughter was bleeding on the ground.

"Fine," I said, looking hard at Allie. *Understand*, I thought desperately. *Work with me, Al.*

I watched her face and thought that she'd understood my silent plea. I saw the way her eyes widened, the way she bent back slightly, ready to release the tension in her knees and drop to the ground at the first possible moment.

I curled my fingers around the handle, ignoring my nerves and my fear. Those emotions could get Allie killed. This was about training—about the fight—and I could do this. I *had* to do this.

I kept my muscles tense and my eyes on the demon. I had to trust that Allie would move when I needed her to. That the demon wouldn't cut first. That this plan would work because, dammit, I didn't have another one.

Shit.

I just had to go for it, and I whipped my hand out—and then was shocked to see something large and cylindrical come soaring toward the demon from off to one side. Before I even had time to process that oddity, it clattered on the pavement just a few inches from the demon. He turned reflexively away from Allie, giving her a few precious milliseconds to drop back from the demon's knife even as I released my own.

I shifted my aim as I threw, and was relieved when the blade sliced open his cheek. I would have preferred to have buried it deep in his eye and ended the creature, but I was willing to take what I could get. And I don't think I have ever heard a more joyous sound than that demon's yowl.

"Allie!" I yelled. "Get out of there!"

My words were completely unnecessary. She was already putting distance between herself and the demon—which wasn't hard considering the demon had obviously changed his mind and was now racing in the opposite direction down the alley.

I was running, too, toward Allie, who I immediately pulled behind me.

"Mom?"

"Are you okay?"

"Yes, but—"

"We're not alone."

"Oh!" She was holding my shoulders and her grip tightened immediately. If the demon hadn't scared her, I knew she would have figured that out all on her own, and I could tell she was irritated with herself for overlooking one simple detail: someone else threw that canister.

And the someone else was still in the alley.

"Show yourself," I said, tensing as a teenage girl with wide, insolent eyes and a mass of dark blonde hair stepped out from the shadows and into the slash of sunlight that filled the center of the alley.

I recognized her immediately—and why wouldn't I? I'd seen her just a few hours before at the market. The girl who'd reminded me of Allie.

"Who the hell are you, and why have you been following me?"

"I'm Eliza," she said simply. "I'm your cousin."

CHAPTER 9

My cousin?

The words seemed to hang in the air, like some absurd cartoon balloon.

It wasn't possible. And yet. . .

And yet damned if some small bubble of hope wasn't building up inside of me. If she was my cousin, then that implied an aunt. An uncle. Maybe even grandparents.

I'd been alone since I was four—loved, yes, but alone, with no clue as to where or who I'd come from.

Could this be real? Or was this another type of demonic knife, designed to twist my heart and throw me off-balance?

I stayed frozen as my mind whirled, and then I cursed myself when Allie stepped around me, her stance defiant. "Gee, Mom," she said to me though her eyes never left Eliza. "Kinda weird that you could have a cousin since, oh, you don't actually have any family." She took three long steps away from me and retrieved my knife that had clattered to the ground. She stood in front of Eliza, feet planted, a fifteen-year-old warrior. "Tell me who you are, or I swear this is going to be over before it starts."

Inside, I cringed. She was doing everything right, and while it made me proud of her, it made me disgusted with myself. I should have been the one handling this. Not my fifteen-year-old daughter.

And yet there she was, stepping in to keep me steady so that I wouldn't be swept away by false hopes and gossamer dreams.

And that's all this was. Hope. Dreams.

Didn't I know better than anyone that the only way to survive in this world was to look reality in the face—and to kick back when it kicked you?

I straightened my shoulders and moved to stand in front of Allie. "I don't know you," I said Eliza. "And if you're going to try to pull that kind of bullshit, you really should do your homework."

"I did," she said, and now her voice was weaker. I guessed that she was eighteen or nineteen, but right then she looked as young as Allie, and when she spoke again, her chin trembled slightly, the way Allie's did when she was fighting back tears. "I did do my homework," she said. "My mom was your mom's little sister."

"No," I said, shaking my head slowly. My chest felt heavy, my throat thick.

"I can prove it," she said.

"Bullshit," Allie said, even as the girl slowly—as slowly as if I were a bomb about to go off—reached toward the collar of her shirt. "*Don't.*"

Allie's single word came out harsh and full of dark promises.

"It's okay," I said.

"Okay? She could have a weapon hidden in her bra."

But I'd seen the thin chain around her neck, and I was certain that it held something important. Something currently hidden beneath her shirt. "Let her," I said. "Stay on guard, but let her."

In front of us, Eliza had frozen. Now she continued, moving painfully slowly as she tugged on the chain and withdrew a small golden locket.

"Take it off," I said. "Take it off and toss it here."

"I'm not throwing it. It's old. And it's all I have left."

I told myself I knew better. That I shouldn't be taken in by the tears. But she looked at me with eyes that resembled Allie's, and it was all I could do not to hold out my arms to draw her in. To comfort her.

I wanted to believe—and that scared me to death.

"Take it off," I said, forcing an edge into my voice. "Put it on the ground, then back away five steps."

She kept her eyes on mine, her teeth gnawing at her lower lip. Then she nodded—just one quick tilt of her head. Her hands reached back, slowly and easily, and she unfastened the necklace. Then she backed away.

All the while, Allie stood watching, her stance ready, her hand tight on the knife.

"Get it," I said to Allie, pointing toward the necklace. She scurried forward, snatched it up, then delivered it to me. "Open it," I said.

She hesitated, but I nodded. Whatever was in that locket affected both of us.

As I kept my eyes on Eliza, Allie slid her fingernail down the locket seam. She pulled the two heart-shaped sides apart, and I heard her sharp intake of breath. "Mom," she said, her voice little more than a whisper.

I glanced down—then felt my heart twist at the two images that filled up the spaces in the locket. Two women. One who looked remarkably like the girl standing in front of me. And the other so familiar that I might have been looking in a mirror.

"Where did you get this?" I asked. My voice was harsh. Raw. Unrecognizable even to my own ears.

"Mom?"

But I ignored Allie, instead taking a step toward the girl. It was midafternoon, but I felt lost in the dark. I was a grown-up. A mother, a wife. But I felt four years old all over again. "*Tell me*," I demanded. "Tell me where you got this."

I could barely speak through the tears that rose in my throat, and I felt suddenly weak. A cold anger rose all around me, and I wasn't sure if it was directed at the girl, at the woman in the picture, at *Forza*, or at the twist of fate that had left me an orphan. All I knew was that the foundation of the earth had been yanked out from under me and I was tumbling fast through space.

I don't remember falling to the ground, but the next thing I knew, I was on my knees.

I'd lost my grip—and thank god Allie was there to take charge.

I don't know when she'd managed it, but she'd left my side and crept up close to Eliza. Now she moved with remarkable swiftness and got her knife up against the girl's throat.

"*Allie.*"

"No," she said fiercely. "No, we do this smart." She licked her lips and lifted her chin, and I saw guts and determination. Right then, she was taking care of me—and we both knew it.

"Okay," I said.

"Okay," she repeated with a sharp nod. "We're going back to the B&B. We're going back and we're going to figure this out. And you," she added, taking the knife away but poking Eliza with her finger, "you are coming with us."

I may have been unsteady, but I got to my feet. Allie was doing great, but no way was I allowing her to run this show. If Eliza was a risk, I didn't want Allie at the front line any more than she already was. And if Eliza really was family—well, I wanted to hedge my bets.

I waved my fingers, indicating she should come over. She did, albeit tentatively, and with Allie practically glued to her side.

"You may be who you say you are," I acknowledged. "But I'm not taking any chances. Arms up," I said, and when she complied, I patted her down. I found a razor in her bra—score a point for Allie—and a switchblade tucked inside her ankle-high boots. Other than that, she was clean.

I slid the switchblade into my pocket and the razor into my purse. "All right," I said, heading out of the alley to circle back around to the restaurant—and to Stuart and Timmy. "Let's go."

"Mom," Allie said, and I could hear the question in her voice plain enough.

"We have to tell him," I said by way of answer. "We have to tell him everything."

I don't know if Eliza understood that I was talking about my husband, or if she was even curious. But to her credit, she stayed quiet. When we arrived back at the café, Stuart was bent over and strapping Timmy into the stroller.

"Jesus, Kate," he said, his expression a mix of relief and irritation. "I was just about to call the embassy. Either that or. . ." He trailed off with a shrug, his eyes narrowed at Eliza. But it didn't matter—I knew well enough the word he didn't speak. *Forza.*

"That second option would have been the right place to call," I said wryly as I looked pointedly at Eliza. "Apparently this is going to be more of a working vacation than I'd planned."

"Oh." His eyes darted from me to Eliza. "Is she a—you know?"

It was a good question, and I suddenly felt like a bit of an idiot since the possibility that Eliza was a demon hadn't occurred to me before. Just another clue that the girl's claim that she was family had messed me up more than I wanted to admit.

I started to say that I didn't think so, but couldn't be sure, when Allie whipped out the spray bottle of holy water I keep in Timmy's diaper bag and squirted Eliza in the face.

All around us, the restaurant patrons' eyes widened, and I was pretty sure I heard someone mutter "Crazy Americans" in muffled Italian.

But since crazy Americans come to the Spanish Steps all the time, we weren't worth more than a cursory glance, especially since Eliza's skin didn't start to sizzle and pop.

"Wow," Eliza said in a voice that dripped sarcasm. "That was pretty refreshing on such a hot day."

I aimed a frown toward Stuart. "No," I said. "Not a you-know-what. Which is good," I added. "Because I think she might be my cousin."

His eyes widened with surprise, and I steeled for—for what?

I didn't know, but I immediately felt guilty because my expectation was that Stuart would muddy the waters and make an already tense situation even more uncomfortable.

He didn't, though. Instead, he stepped up to the plate.

"All right then," he said, dropping a wad of euros on the table to cover the minimal check. "In that case, let's get somewhere we can talk, and we'll figure out just exactly what is going on."

"The B&B," Allie said.

"No," Stuart and I said together. I cocked my head and smiled at him, feeling a bit like maybe, just maybe, we were becoming a team.

"Um, why not?" Allie asked.

"If she's not who she says she is," Stuart said, "we don't want her knowing where we're staying."

"It's not like they don't already know," Allie said and then winced as Stuart narrowed his eyes at me.

"*They?*" he repeated.

"Sorry," Allie said.

"Kate?" Stuart's voice was rough. And, I thought, just a little hurt.

"I've been meaning to bring you up to speed," I said. "There are a few things to tell you."

"I see."

I bit back a grimace. Yes, I was definitely hearing hurt and anger.

To Stuart's credit, he sucked it up and pressed on. "Maybe *they* do know. But that doesn't mean we need to advertise our location any more than necessary."

From beside Allie, Eliza let out a long-suffering sigh. "Oh, give it a rest. We might as well go back there. It's not like I don't know already know."

I narrowed my eyes at her. "Oh, really. Where, then?"

"Well, duh," she said, with an Allie-like roll of her eyes. "You're in the room next to mine." She dropped that bombshell at the exact moment that Timmy grabbed the tablecloth and gave it a tug, sending all the plates and cutlery clattering to the ground.

Honestly, this was not one of my better days.

I glanced toward Stuart, who looked more irritated with me than he did with our son. To be honest, I can't say I was surprised.

"*Soon*," he mouthed to me, and I nodded, feeling chastised and guilty and confused. The guilt came from the simple knowledge that he was right.

The confusion from the sudden and unpleasant realization that although I told myself that I wanted and hoped for Stuart to be an active and willing participant in this unusual life of mine, when it got down to the wire, I really just wanted to go it alone.

Except that wasn't true either. More and more, I wanted Allie at my side. And the deep, dark, completely honest truth was that despite everything that had happened with Eric, he was the partner I truly wanted watching my back.

For so long, I'd feared Stuart's reaction when he learned the truth about me. Because when I'd married him, I'd simply been Kate. Not Kate the Demon Hunter. Just Kate the single mom, trying to get past her grief and get on with her life.

Considering he'd left—twice—I'd been right to worry. But maybe it wasn't Stuart's reaction I should have been focused on. Because while Kate the Wife and Mom loved Stuart unconditionally, Kate the Demon Hunter would never have fallen in love with Stuart in the first place. And with every moment that we were back in Rome—with every memory and every danger—that unpleasant and horrible truth was bearing down on me.

And, yes, I could keep running—could keep looking in the opposite direction and hope that it would go away. But eventually, I knew that I would have to deal with that, and I wasn't sure I knew how. I could drive a spike through the eye of a demon to save myself and my family. But how the hell did I save a relationship?

My thoughts meandered through those dark hallways as we walked the brightly lit streets of Rome. Me, two teenagers, my husband, and our toddler son. If Stuart knew the direction of my thoughts, he hid it well. He concentrated on pushing the stroller and keeping his eyes on Eliza. He was alert and focused, and in that moment I thought that maybe it would all turn out okay. That maybe he could be an asset, even if he wasn't a full partner.

I frowned, wondering if I'd discovered the source of my hesitations. Maybe it wasn't that I didn't want to be Kate the Demon Hunter with Stuart. Maybe it was that I was afraid of losing him altogether if he became drawn into this life. Pushing him away might hurt, but in the end it might just keep him alive.

He glanced at me and his brows lifted when he saw me watching him. He shot a meaningful look at Eliza. "Problem?" he whispered.

I shook my head. "No. Just thinking." I reached for his hand. "I'll tell you later." And as I spoke those words, I knew that I meant them. Whatever dark thoughts about my marriage were circling my head, my husband had a right to know. Maybe they'd hurt. Maybe they'd help. But I owed the truth to this man with whom I'd exchanged sacred vows.

We walked two by three. The girls in front, where I could keep an eye on Eliza, and Stuart and me in the back with Timmy rolling along in front of us, powered by Stuart's push and the wheels of the stroller.

Despite my wandering thoughts, I was keeping a close eye on Allie and her companion. Close enough that I saw the dark-haired demon from the market a full two seconds before she tackled Eliza from the side, landing on top of her—a knife to her neck—and sending Allie sprawling.

Those two seconds saved Eliza's life. I leaped forward, then thrust out with my foot. My comfy Keds intersected with the woman's wrist, sending the knife flying and Eliza's attacker reeling sideways.

Eliza gasped and took the opportunity to scramble backwards, crab-like, even as Allie lunged for the knife. "Mom!" she cried, tossing it to me.

I was already over the woman's chest, my legs pinning her arms to her side. I released my grip on her neck long enough to catch the knife, then started to thrust it down toward her eye.

"*Kate!*"

Stuart's cry startled me, giving the demon the opportunity to lurch up. Her forehead connected with mine, and I rocked backward. She jerked her arms free, then shoved me back. "Fool," she snarled as she leapt to her feet and bolted.

Allie started to run after her, and I held off on cursing Stuart to yell for her to stop.

"But Mom!" she protested, skidding to a stop.

"Let her go," Stuart said, before I could get a word in.

"What the *hell* were you thinking?" I demanded.

"Me?" he asked, sweeping his arm out to indicate the crowd that had gathered around us. "I'm really not interested in posting bail in Italy. Especially since I'm not even sure if you can post bail in Italy."

Shit. He was right, of course. I'd been so caught up in the moment—the attack, the possibility of losing Eliza before I knew her story, the whole damn thing—that I'd completely ignored the fact that we had an audience.

"Right," I said. I climbed to my feet and held out a hand to help Eliza up. "Right. Sorry. You're right."

Stuart came up and took me in his arms. "It's going to be okay," he whispered.

I tilted my head back to look at my husband—and desperately wished that I believed him.

CHAPTER 10

"So do you think it's true?" Stuart asked me.

We'd arrived back at the B&B, and Stuart had pulled me into the hallway just outside our room. Inside, Eliza sat on the bed and Allie stood guard. The door was cracked, and I could see my daughter, diligent and wary, with the knife tight in her hand. Timmy was safe and sound in the room he shared with Allie, asleep in his portable playpen, the TV playing softly to keep him company if he woke up.

"Is she related to you?" Stuart pressed.

I ran a hand through my hair. "How the hell do I know? For that matter, how the hell *can* I know? Am I supposed to run a DNA test?" The words snapped out of me, and I immediately regretted them. "Sorry," I said with more calm than I felt. "This has kind of thrown me."

"Me, too," he said. He sighed, then held out his arms. I moved into them gratefully. "Whatever you need, I'm here," he said. He held me tight for a moment, then eased gently away. With one finger, he tilted my chin up. "Soon, though. Soon, we're going to talk."

"I know," I said. "Right now, it's her we need to talk to." I glanced back into the room and took a deep breath. Then I held out my hand for Stuart. For his support. For his love. "You'll stand with me?"

"Always," he said, and we went into the room together.

Eliza looked up when we entered. "I get that you don't believe me," she said. "After all the stuff I've seen growing up, believe me, I get it. But it's true. And—" Her voice broke and she looked away. Her skin turned splotchy in what I recognized as the familiar warning sign of oncoming tears. But she backed it off, took a deep breath, and started to talk. When she did, her voice was remarkably level, and I felt a twist of almost maternal pride.

"It's okay," Allie said. She slid down so that she was sitting on the floor, her back against the wall. She still held the knife, but it was clear that, like me, she was softening toward this girl. "Just tell us and we'll go from there."

Allie's words resonated with me, and I glanced at Stuart. *Just tell him how I feel. Just tell him, and we'd go from there.*

Not now, though. Right now was about Eliza. And as I moved to sit on the floor next to Allie, the girl on the bed who looked so much like my daughter started to tell her tale.

"You didn't really know your mom, right?" she asked, peering at me.

"No," I admitted. "I don't remember her at all."

She nodded as if she'd expected the answer, but it was a moment before she spoke again, and it took all my effort not to fill the silence. To tell her how I'd been four years old and wandering the streets of Rome. I wanted to say that, but I didn't. Because if she was who she said she was, then she should know some of that already.

"Your mom's name was Amanda," she said. "Did you know that?"

I shook my head, hoping I looked calm despite the way my heart was twisting.

"She was my mom's sister. My mom's Deborah, by the way, but everyone calls her Debbie."

"My aunt," I said, the word so soft I wasn't sure I'd spoken it aloud.

Eliza nodded. "They were pretty far apart in age. Your mom was in her early twenties when she died. Twenty-four, I think. My mom was sixteen."

I nodded, trying to keep it all straight in my head. "Go on."

"Well, anyway, apparently our grandmother— yours and mine, I mean—was a Demon Hunter."

I cocked my head. Surely if that were true Father Corletti would have told me. He may not have known who my parents were when I'd first come to *Forza*, but he'd learned recently about the connection between my parents and Eric's. Surely he would have learned this, too?

Eliza must have read my mind because she shrugged. "She wasn't working for *Forza* when your mom was killed. I don't think she had been for a long time."

"Rogue?" I asked. A lot of Hunters were rogue. Most were simply people who knew the truth. They understood that demons walked the earth, and they'd made it their mission to hunt. Some were loosely organized, but most worked on their own. I'd believed that my parents fell into that category. Just two people who knew about the darkness that mars our world, and had made it their mission to step up and fight.

"I think so," Eliza said. "But I think she was with *Forza* when she was younger."

"You think?"

Eliza shrugged. "She died when I was pretty little."

"A demon?" Allie whispered.

"No. Cancer. She'd been out of it. No hunting, no nothing. At least as far as I know."

"All right," I said, still trying to wrap my head around all of this. "So our grandmother died when you were little. But you knew her?"

Eliza nodded. "Oh, yeah. We lived just down the street from her in San Diego. She'd make pancakes every Sunday."

I glanced at Allie and saw that she was biting her lower lip. She had grandparents—Stuart's mom and dad. But they weren't her blood kin. They loved her, but I knew she felt the difference. The loss.

I knew because I felt it, too.

"Anyway, I guess I'm getting off track. The point is that she—Grandma, I mean—wasn't hunting when I was little. She never said, but I think that's how my grandfather died. I never knew him. I think they hunted together and he died and she retired. I mean, that happens a lot, right?" She looked at me and then at Stuart, then back to me again.

I hadn't retired because Eric died on the job, but I nodded anyway. What she described wasn't my path, but I knew that it was a common one.

"Anyway, back in the day, I guess that Amanda got all wrapped up in the demon hunting thing. My mom was a lot younger, and wasn't interested or else she didn't know about it—I'm not sure. But I know that Amanda met a guy and they had a kid. She was pretty young. My age, I think. I'm eighteen," she added, which confirmed my earlier guess.

"I'm the kid?" I asked, my throat tight. "Or do I have a sibling out there somewhere?" Just thinking about the possibility made my chest hurt. At my side, Allie gripped my wrist, but whether to comfort me or herself, I didn't know.

"No, just you," Eliza said. "And when you were about four, Amanda and Todd—that's my uncle, your dad, I mean—well, they got deep into some sort of demon shit."

"Todd," I said, letting the name roll over my tongue. My father's name was Todd.

She cocked her head to look at me. "So, like, all of this is new to you? Honest?"

"Keep going," I said, deflecting the question. Most of it was new, yes. But I did know that my parents were in the middle of a big demon-y mess when they were killed. I knew because Eric knew. Because my parents had been killed trying to stop his parents from performing a ritual to bind a demon inside him.

My parents had failed—and that demon had burst free just a few months ago, nearly destroying Eric in the process.

All those years ago, my parents had apparently left me in a ratty motel while they went off to hunt. I'd always believed that I'd simply been an anonymous lost child wandering the streets of Rome. Now I know that was a story that Father Donnelly, one of the priests high enough up the food chain to know about *Forza*, had told Father Corletti who then, as now, was in charge of overseeing *Forza Scura*, the secret branch within the Vatican charged with hunting, destroying, and studying the demonic forces that move about in our world.

Like me, Father Corletti believed I was simply an orphan, possibly abandoned by my vacationing American parents. I was raised in a church-run orphanage, then indoctrinated into *Forza* even before I'd reached puberty, doing research first and then later tracking and taking out demons in the field.

I'd only recently learned that my parents had lived that life, too. Instead, I'd spent my youth imagining them as simply average Americans. In my mind, my mother stayed at home to tend to me, reading me books like *Curious George* and *Goodnight Moon*. My father owned a gas station— I'm not sure why that caught my childhood imagination, but it did—and would come home smelling of grease and Irish Spring soap. He'd pick me up and kiss me and swing me around until I was perched on his shoulders. They hadn't abandoned me, of course. As far as my imagination was concerned, they'd been brutally attacked by a vile mugger, much like the origin story behind Bruce Wayne's transformation into Batman. With her last dying breath, my mother had told me to run, and I had, only to be rescued, both literally and figuratively, by the Church.

It was a fantasy that had been surprisingly comforting as a child.

It was a fantasy that I found all too hard to give up, even now that I knew the truth.

"Kate?"

I glanced at Stuart, only then realizing that he'd come to sit on the floor on the other side of me so that I was now sandwiched between my husband and my daughter. He took my hand, his expression one of deep concern.

"I'm okay," I said. "This is all just a bit . . . much."

Eliza pulled her knees up to her chest, her bare feet on the bed cover. "I'm sorry," she said, as she hugged her legs tight. "I didn't mean to—"

"No," I said. "I want to hear. I'm glad to hear." I drew in a breath. "Tell me more."

She licked her lips, her eyes darting to Allie before she continued. She was three years older than my daughter and was traveling through Rome on her own. Eliza was an adult, albeit a young one. But I could still see the little girl inside her. And yes, my heart was melting just a little. Despite telling myself that I needed to be cold—that I needed to be careful—I could feel myself warming up.

More important, I could feel myself believing.

"Really," I urged gently. "I'm glad you're here. I'm glad you're telling me this."

She drew in a breath as she hugged her knees tighter. "It's just that—it's just that I wanted so bad to meet you, you know? Once my mom told me to find you."

I caught Allie's eye. "Your mom knew about me?"

She nodded. "Yeah, she—" Eliza cut herself off. "It's easier if I tell the whole story in order. Okay?"

"Sure," Allie said before I could answer. "We just want to hear."

"Right. Okay. So, like I said, your mom and dad were here. On the trail of some demon. I don't know the details. I don't think my mom did, either."

Did. The word seemed to fill the room, and I suddenly felt cold. I steeled myself, though, and said nothing. I wanted the story, not grief or explanations. And, yes, I wanted this unknown aunt to live in Eliza's words for as long as she could. Because if she was dead, that reality would strike me soon enough.

"Was your mom here, too? Your grandma?" Allie asked.

"No. They were both back in San Diego. Like I said, my grandma was out of the demon thing, and my mom was only sixteen. So she was just doing school. But then—well, then they disappeared. Todd and Amanda, I mean. They just seemed to fall off the planet, and you along with them."

"Did they look?" Allie asked.

Eliza shrugged. "I guess Grandma thought they went into hiding or something. Honest, I'm kinda fuzzy on the details. Maybe she figured they'd been killed—and you, too—or maybe she was looking and just couldn't find anything out. But my mom wasn't in the loop. I mean, she was younger than I am now, and that wasn't her life. Not really. Not then. But when my mom was in college—San Diego State—she found all this stuff about *Forza* and demons and everything when she was helping Grandma sort out all the junk in her garage."

"She asked questions and then took up the family business," Stuart said wryly.

Eliza nodded. "She wanted to know what happened to her sister. And I guess somewhere along the way it ended up being just as much about fighting the demons."

I grimaced. "That has a way of happening. Once you see evil, it's hard not to fight it."

"I get that," Eliza said. "I've been doing it pretty much my whole life."

"Who's your father?" Stuart asked.

She lifted a shoulder. "His name was Max. He was a Hunter, too. She met him about five years after she started hunting and had me when she was just shy of thirty. I guess Grandma had been training her, and then Max took over and they worked together. Then they had me." Another lift of her shoulder. "He died in the line, you know? But it's not the kind of job where they give you a medal."

"No," I said. "It's not." I stood up and went to look out the window. The day was clear, and I could hear the laughter of children playing in the street and the din of traffic as the cars and trucks moved from place to place. "Why didn't they join *Forza?*"

"I'm not entirely sure," Eliza said. "I'm not—I mean, I've been working with my mom for years, but she's never been much for oversharing, you know?"

"I get that," Allie said, and I turned from the window to scowl at her.

"Excuse me? You are so much more in the loop than you should be."

Allie looked at Eliza and rolled her eyes, the gesture so genuine and spontaneous I almost laughed out loud.

From the look on Eliza's face, I think she almost did, too. "Anyway, once I was born, she ratcheted back the hunting. We had a house close to Grandma, and she'd watch me when Mom went away—I learned later she was off hunting. And I learned that she'd been poking around about Amanda and Todd and you for years. I know she must have gotten some solid intel because she started to plan a trip here. And she even contacted *Forza*—I mean, she's talked to them before, so that wasn't a huge leap. She may have been rogue, but not secretly rogue, if you know what I mean."

"I get it. Go on."

"That's pretty much it," Eliza said. She licked her lips, then looked down at her hands that she was twisting around in her lap. "And then just over a week ago there was—there was an accident," she said. Her eyes glittered with tears. "A truck ran a red light, and—"

She cut herself off and shook her head violently. "Anyway, she was in the hospital, but she was too messed up. She didn't make it."

"Eliza," I said. It was all I could manage. Already the room was swimming through my eyes, too. Already, I could barely feel the pressure of Stuart's hand tightening around mine.

"She was groggy, you know? Drugged up. But she told me this stuff—the stuff about you, I mean. I already knew about the hunting. She's been training me since I was a kid. And she told me to find you." Her shoulders rose and fell. Then she lifted her head and met my eyes. "She told me I had to, because you're the only family I have left. Please," she added. "You have to believe me. I don't have any place else to go."

"So, *do* you believe her?" Stuart asked, parroting the question he'd asked me more than an hour ago.

"Do you?" I asked.

We were in the hall—well away from the closed door so that we couldn't be overheard. And, of course, the simple fact that I had left Allie in that room with Eliza went a long way to answering Stuart's question.

He reached out and stroked my hair, but he didn't answer me. I knew why. The answer affected all of us, but I was the one who had to make the first decision as to whether or not to trust her.

From somewhere behind us, I heard the pat of footsteps. I turned, intending to tell Allie to stay in the room with Eliza. But it wasn't Allie approaching—it was Mrs. Micari.

"*Signora*," I said. "Good afternoon."

She smiled, but I thought it was a little too wide and a little too bright. "You would like the afternoon snacks? Wine for the parents? Or perhaps coffee? And the biscotti for the younger ones? I serve downstairs now. Please, come and sit with me. Tell me about your day. You have met Eliza, no? I saw you come in with her."

"We did," I said. "How well do you know her?"

Mrs. Micari laughed. "Not at all. But I cannot help but feel like a grandmother to one so young who travels alone. Please, come. I will serve in ten minutes?"

I hesitated, then nodded. I'm not sure why I was reluctant. All I knew was that I wanted answers, and I wouldn't be getting them over wine and biscotti. "Thank you," I said. "I'm sure we'd all love some."

She beamed at me, then hurried back downstairs. I watched her go, then shrugged at Stuart. "I don't know about you, but I could use some wine."

"I bet you could," he said gently. He said nothing after that. I knew he wasn't going to press. But I also knew that he wanted an answer.

"Yes," I finally said. "Yes, I believe her. The heart of it, anyway."

His eyes narrowed, and I saw the wheels turning. Stuart's an attorney, and though he may not deal with criminals, he understands deception. "She's evading," he said. "At least a little bit."

"A little bit?" I countered. "She hasn't addressed the big questions at all. How she came to be here. How exactly she ended up in my B&B. And why didn't she talk to me right off the bat?

"You believe her," Stuart said. "But you don't trust her."

I thought about what Eric said—*don't trust anyone.*

"I want to," I admitted. "But I don't."

"You need to ask her the hard questions, Kate." He reached out and curled a lock of my hair around his finger, his eyes never leaving mine. "Do you want me to take Allie out? Give you the chance to talk to Eliza alone?"

I considered it for a moment, then shook my head. "No. This is about all of us." And, honestly, it was about Eric, too. But I couldn't go there.

I sighed then leaned in and brushed a kiss over his lips. "I'm sorry," I said.

His eyes were soft, but knowing. "What for?"

"For the things in my head," I said, drawing a breath as I hoped not to drown in these marital waters. I tilted my head down and spoke to the floor. "For not knowing in my heart that you're strong enough to deal with this. For not believing that we can be a team in this new life I've dumped all over us."

I licked my lips, then forced myself to meet his eyes. "I've been pissed, Stuart. Maybe I haven't shown it. Or maybe you've just been giving me space. But there's been this anger bubbling underneath."

He stayed silent, but he didn't look angry himself. He didn't even look hurt. Instead, he looked both attentive and understanding, and that gave me the strength to go on.

"It broke me when you left, and part of the reason Allie and I were coming here was to heal. And then when you showed up at the house—"

"I messed up your plans."

"Yes. No." I waved a hand as if that would somehow wipe the confusion away. "Both, honestly. It was a miracle that you came back, and I wouldn't trade that moment for anything. But it didn't erase the hurt. And it hasn't been that long, and I'm still processing. And that's why—" I sucked in a long, deep breath. "That's why I've kept you out of the loop. All the stuff that's happened so far—the demon-y stuff, I mean—I kept you out because I wasn't sure I wanted you in at all."

His expression was unreadable. This was the face of the attorney. The negotiator. It was a face he rarely wore with me, and I shifted uncomfortably, wishing I knew what he was thinking, and fearing the worst.

"You don't have anything to be sorry about," he said gently. "I gave you reason not to trust me."

"Yeah," I said. "You did. But I'm not innocent, either. I waited way too long to tell you the truth. I should have told you everything when that first demon crashed through the window."

"Maybe," he said. "Or maybe we should forget about blame and just move forward."

I nodded. "I'd like that. No," I corrected. "I *want* that."

"Do you? Because you said you *weren't* sure you wanted me in the loop. Does that mean you're sure now?"

I started to say yes, then forced myself to stop. "Do you want my honest answer?"

"That's all I've ever wanted, Kate."

"Then the answer is that I don't know. I want to be sure," I added quickly. "I want us to be a team. I really do. But I'm afraid it's never going to—"

"To be the way it was with Eric."

"I know that sounds horrible," I said. "But yeah."

"It doesn't have to be the same. And how could it? You two hunted together for years. I can barely throw a knife. But we can find our own rhythm, Kate. Hell, we *need* to find our own rhythm. Do you think I want to be Eric's clone?" he asked, his voice dripping with irony.

"I'm going to go with no," I said. I rose up on my toes to kiss him again. "And that's a good thing."

"Is it?"

I heard the uncertainty in his voice, and it made my heart twist. "It is," I said. "I loved him—I still love him. You know that. But that doesn't mean I love you less."

"Just different."

"Please, Stuart. You know how hard it is."

"I do," he said. "Nothing messes people up more than family." His mouth curved into a wry grin. "Except maybe love."

I laughed. "Isn't that the truth?"

He glanced pointedly toward the closed door to our bedroom, and I understood that we were shifting our conversation. "I'm sorry about your aunt. About your parents."

"It doesn't matter," I said as I moved into Stuart's open arms, my eyes closed tight to ward off the threatening tears. "I never knew them. They never existed to me. This doesn't really change anything."

Except that was a lie. It changed everything . . . and we both knew it.

CHAPTER 11

"Wait, wait," Eliza was saying as we walked back into the room. "Show me again."

Allie stood in the middle of the room wearing my favorite leather jacket. As far as I could tell, neither girl had noticed our return. Instead, Eliza was focused on Allie and Allie was wrapped up in her demonstration.

She had her arm up, but now she extended it quickly, causing the stiletto that Eric had once given me to slide out from under the interior cuff. "Isn't it cool? Mom rigged it up, but there's a jacket in one of the stores down the street, and I'm sure I can do the same thing if—*Mom*."

"You can do the same thing if . . .?" I prompted with my brows raised. "Since when did you learn to sew?"

She dragged her teeth across her lower lip. "I could probably learn. Or you could do it for me. I mean, it's *so* handy. And a Demon Hunter needs the proper tools, right? Just like I can't do geometry without a protractor or chemistry without the periodic table."

I felt my lips twitch, but managed not to smile.

"It really is cool, Mrs. Connor," Eliza said.

"Kate," I said. "I may be old enough to be your mom, but cousins call each other by their first names."

"You believe me," she said, her body visibly relaxing.

"I guess I do. But there are still things I need to know." I nodded toward the bed. "Sit.".

She complied and I turned to Allie. "Well?"

Her brow furrowed. "Um . . . what?"

"How about you? Do you believe her?"

She cocked her head, looking between me and Eliza. "Is this like a test?"

"Maybe."

She rolled her eyes, but stood straight. "Fine. Okay. Yeah, I believe her." She looked from me to Eliza. "Except . . . " She trailed off with a shrug, then turned back to me.

"Except what?" Eliza said, before I had the chance to. On the far side of the room, Stuart settled into the pretty, upholstered arm chair, his eyes on Allie.

"Except it doesn't all quite fit," Allie said. When neither Eliza nor I said anything, she continued. "I mean, we're in Rome. It's not like we live here. So how'd you find us? It couldn't be a coincidence, right, Mom?" At my nod, she continued. "And you said you were looking for us—for Mom—and you got here before us. But then you didn't say anything once we arrived? You didn't even tell Mrs. Micari that you wanted to meet us. So, I mean, what's up with that?"

She turned back to me. "And, well, like that. It's all just a little off."

"She's right," I said, looking at Eliza. "And just so we're clear, I *do* believe you. You can't manufacture a family resemblance like the one we have. We're related. But believing you and trusting you are two different things. And we're not quite to trust yet."

"You left me alone with Allie," she said with the kind of teenage defiance I was becoming more and more familiar with as Allie grew older.

"Don't make me regret that," I said sharply. Then I softened my tone to add, "And you and I both know that there are all kinds of trust. If you'd wanted either of us dead, you've had plenty of time to do it. Hell, that demon in the alley behind the restaurant would have done it for you."

"Maybe I'm working with him," she said. "Maybe he and I had it all planned out so that I could gain your trust."

"Maybe," I admitted. I moved to the bed and sat beside her, my body turned slightly so that I could face her. It gave me a good view of Stuart, too, and I could see the irritation on his face. He hadn't yet heard about the old man in the alley, and I added that to my mental list of things to come clean about.

Right now, though, my focus was on the girl. "Do you want to tell us the rest? Or do you want to nurse hurt feelings because I'm not wrapping my arms around you and swearing that everything you say is golden?"

"I called Father Donnelly," she said, looking at her hands in her lap.

She spoke softly. Even so, the words hit me with the force of a slap. "He *knew*? He's known I'm related to your mom?"

"No!" The word came out so fast and so harsh that I believed her. "At least—at least, I don't think he knew."

Father Donnelly was one of the priests who worked inside of *Forza*. He was, in fact, the priest most likely to take over after Father Corletti retired, and that was not a day that I was looking forward to.

It was hard for me not to trust a priest, but Father Donnelly rubbed me the wrong way, and he always had. It had only gotten worse since I learned that he was the *alimentatore* who worked with Eric's parents. The man within *Forza* who helped trap a demon inside Eric with the hope that they would be creating a Hunter with unique skills and insight.

To say that little plan went horribly wrong would be an understatement. And no matter how much Father Donnelly's heart might have been in the right place, there was no getting around the fact that his reckless Frankenstein games with the man who would later be my husband also resulted in the death of my parents. Because it was Amanda and Todd who had gone after Eric's parents in an aborted attempt to stop the ceremony. And when it was all over, both Eric and I had been orphaned.

So, no. I was not a Father Donnelly fan. And right then, I couldn't help but wonder what he had told Eliza—and why.

"Just spit it out," Allie said to Eliza, though her eyes were on me.

"It's just that I'd met him before. I told you that Mom trained me. And even though she was rogue, she'd talked with *Forza* about working with them. So after Mom died, I called him. I told him what I'd learned when I went through Mom's stuff. And I told him that she said I needed to find you."

"Find me? All that, and she didn't know where I was?"

"She probably did, but I couldn't find it anywhere," Eliza said. "Father Donnelly told me that you lived in San Diablo, but that you were coming to Rome and where you'd be staying. That's all." Her lower lip trembled. "This all just happened, Kate. I've been—well, I've been a little messed up, you know?"

"All right," I said more gently. "But why didn't you say something right away?"

She licked her lips, then looked at her hands. "Because of Mom's notes. Because of the things she wrote about your husband. She wasn't sure she trusted him, and so I wasn't sure I should trust you."

I glanced at Stuart, but that was only a reflex. I knew that Eliza meant Eric. If Debbie had been investigating my parents, it made sense that she'd learned about what had happened when Eric was a kid. And if she had moles within *Forza*, it also made sense that she would have learned that Eric was alive and well and in the body of another man—and had spent a horrific few months battling the demon inside him.

"You shut your mouth," Allie said, her voice a low, violent whisper. "Shut up and take it back. *They're* the ones who messed up my dad. Some stupid faction inside *Forza*. And he fought, and he won. So you just shut the hell up!"

There were tears in her eyes, and I went to her and pulled her into my arms. "She's right," I said to Eliza. "Eric has done nothing but fight demons his entire life." I looked at her hard, silently challenging her to contradict me.

"I'm sorry," she said softly. "But how could I have known?"

"If your mother had done as much research as you said, she should have known," Allie said, but I pressed my hand gently over hers. I wanted to agree, but the truth was that if Debbie had been watching Eric, she might have seen the demon come out. In the end, Eric had won, yes. But someone looking at him through snapshots in time might not have realized that.

Or they might not believe it.

"It's okay," I told Eliza gently. "You trust me now?"

She nodded, then looked to me and Allie in turn. "I really am sorry."

To her credit, Allie lifted a shoulder. "A Hunter has to be careful, I guess."

Eliza's smile spread wide, making her look even more like Allie than before. "That's right," she said.

I reached into my pocket and pulled out her locket. I held it out to her, the fragile chain dangling from my fingertip. She took it eagerly, then fastened it around her neck. "Thanks. I really don't want to lose it."

"I know," I said. I tilted my head to indicate the door. "Mrs. Micari is putting on a spread for us downstairs. Why don't you girls go down and dig in? Stuart and I will be along in a bit."

"They want to talk," Allie told Eliza.

"We do," I admitted. "And we want to check on your brother. Go." I waved them toward the door. "And if Mrs. Micari asks, I'd love a coffee. The jet lag is catching up with me."

"Just the jet lag?" Stuart asked, once the girls had left the room.

"Everything," I admitted. "I'm wiped." I dropped down to sit on the edge of the bed. "I want to snuggle with my husband and sleep for a thousand years."

"Sorry, Sleeping Beauty. I can only help with part of that." He came over to sit next to me. "So no going to *Forza* tonight?"

"No. I really am tired. And I want to process everything Eliza told us before I go see Father Corletti. Or Father Donnelly, for that matter."

"You don't trust him," Eric said.

"I used to. Then Eddie said he didn't trust him." Eddie was a retired Demon Hunter who, through a series of wacky misadventures, now lived with us under the guise of being Eric's grandfather. The guise resulting from the fact that I told that little fib, and it stuck. He'd crossed the eighty-year mark, was as curmudgeonly as they come, and I loved him to death.

"Did he say why?"

"No," I admitted. "But I trust Eddie's instincts. And since I later found out that Father Donnelly had worked with Eric's parents on the whole Create-an-Über-Demon-Hunter plan . . . "

"Yeah," Stuart said. "I get it."

"It's been kind of a crappy first day in Rome for you," I said. "I'm sorry."

"You don't have a thing to be sorry about. This is who you are. And being here helps me understand that a little better. Besides," he added brightly, "I saw the Spanish Steps, rode the subway, and had an encounter with a gypsy. Seems like a pretty full day to me."

"Well, when you put it that way," I said, then leaned in to kiss my husband.

"Should we go out for dinner?" he asked, when we broke the kiss. "We could leave Allie here to watch Timmy. Assuming you trust Eliza enough."

"I do," I admitted, though Eric's warning not to trust anyone still plagued me. "And I trust Allie to watch her own back and her brother's. But can I take a rain check?"

"Too tired?" he asked.

"Yes," I said, though that was only half the truth.

"What is it?" he asked, studying my face. Apparently either exhaustion or guilt was eroding my skill at deception.

"It's just that I need to call the States. I should check in with Laura. And with Eddie. And—"

"You want to talk to Eric."

I dropped my gaze. "I'm sorry," I said, though I wasn't entirely sure what I was apologizing for.

"It's okay, Kate. I thought we cleared some of this out earlier. I get it. Really. I understand that Eric's a part of this. Whether I want him to be or not. Whether *you* want him to be or not."

I nodded, then forced a smile. "Some vacation, huh? First demons. Now relatives. I wonder what's going to come next."

"We're together. Whatever happens next, that's really all that matters."

While Stuart when to check on Timmy and then join the girls, I moved toward the window where the cell reception was better and dialed Eric.

My skin seemed to tighten with every ring. I wanted to talk with him—to tell him what had happened. About the demon attacks. About Eliza. About my parents.

I had appreciated having Stuart at my side through everything, but I couldn't lie to myself. Despite the horror and the hell that had battered Eric and me over the last few months, right then— with my past crashing down around me—it was Eric's voice that I needed to hear.

But that wasn't going to happen. The phone simply rang and rang until finally his voice mail kicked in.

I frowned at the phone, then clicked off without leaving a message. Where the hell could he be? If I was the parent left behind while my teen toured Italy, I would be glued to my phone. So why wasn't Eric?

The thought preyed on me, even though I told myself I was worrying for nothing. Probably the battery died. Or he stayed up late hunting and he simply slept through the call.

There was an explanation. There had to be.

And, telling myself that, I firmly shoved thoughts of Eric out of my mind.

I considered going downstairs for the promised biscotti and coffee. Right then I wanted both the caffeine and the carbs with a fiery passion. But I still had work to do, and so I dialed the next number on my list. It would be early in Los Angeles—just around seven a.m.—and while I felt a little guilty about waking Laura, at least I knew that I would catch her at home.

Except I didn't, and that worried me as well. Not only had she not returned my call, but she wasn't answering her phone. And Eric wasn't answering his.

Had something happened? Were demons on the rampage back in Southern California? Had my friends and family been swept away in some horrible, hellish nightmare?

I sucked in a breath and told myself to be calm. Jet lag and exhaustion were playing with my imagination. My best friend was fine. Eric was fine. And if San Diablo had been sucked into a portal to hell, I'm certain it would have made the Italian news.

The thoughts mollified me, but I dialed one more number anyway, then exhaled with relief when Eddie picked up immediately. "Connor residence. Make it snappy, I got popcorn in the microwave."

"Thanks, Eddie," I said, deadpan. "That's exactly the way I want my phone answered."

"Gripe, gripe, gripe," he said, but I could hear the pleasure in his voice. "You all tucked away in Rome? Our girl burned a hole through your credit card yet? Hang on," he added before I could answer. "Damn machine is beeping now."

I waited impatiently while he set the phone down. I heard the clatter of dishes and imagined him dumping popcorn into one of my good ceramic dishes.

"Popcorn instead of a meal?"

He made a grunting noise, and I pictured his caterpillar-like eyebrows forming a V as he stared me down. "You call just to give me grief? Or are you making sure I didn't burn the house down?"

"I have complete faith in you," I said. "And none of the above."

"Well, dammit, girl. That means there's trouble."

I scowled. "Maybe I just called to let you know we arrived safe and sound."

He made a rough noise that might have been a snort.

"A little trouble," I admitted, unable to stifle my smile.

"Ha!"

"But I hate admitting it because it just makes you more smug."

"Not smug," he said. "Clever. Intuitive. Smart as a whip. And damn sexy, too."

"You are all that," I said.

"So what crisis has you paying international cell phone rates? Demons? Or are we living in the pedestrian land of lost luggage?"

"I wish. And not demons, either, although we've encountered a few," I said cryptically. "Mostly I'm calling because it turns out that I have a cousin."

I could tell from the lack of a sarcastic comeback that I'd caught his attention. "All right," he finally said. "I'm listening."

I gave him the quick and dirty run-down.

"So you're looking for my input about the kid? Or you want me to track down your gal-pal and Snugglemuffins?"

"If you have insight on the kid, I'd love to hear it. And yes, I want to track down Laura and Eric." For the sake of both peace and my sanity, I decided to ignore the Snugglemuffins comment.

"I haven't got a clue about your man, but Laura's off playing footsy with your *sensai.*"

"Oh, really?" My brows rose with interest. Laura had been dating Cutter—aka Sean, aka my martial arts coach—for a while now. "And where exactly are they?"

"Exactly? I don't know. But I'm guessing under the covers in some fancy hotel. Went out about six last night. And the gal still hasn't made it home."

"And you know this how?"

"Because I'm watching the munchkin. What? Allie didn't tell you?"

"I made Allie stop texting," I said. "So if Mindy sent her any gossip she wouldn't share it with me, because then I'd know she broke the rule. Plus, we've been kind of busy battling the forces of evil and meeting new relatives."

He exhaled loudly, the sound reminding me of a snuffling horse. "You watch your back around that one."

"I know," I said, although I had to silently admit that I hadn't been acting like I knew. Instead, I'd been acting like she was a second daughter. Well, maybe I wasn't *quite* that careless, but I'd definitely let down my guard.

"I'm not just talking good sense, girlie," he said, and his voice had taken on a more serious tone. "If she's calling Father Donnelly, then I don't trust her."

"She called the only person she knew to call," I said.

Eddie just snorted.

I sighed. He was right. I was making excuses for this girl, and I didn't even know her. She might be blood, but at the end of the day, that didn't count for much.

"You keep an eye on her," Eddie said. "Especially since she's been around at least twice when demons have taken a run for you."

"You think there's a connection," I said.

"What? You just fall off the turnip truck? Of course there's a connection."

"I'm not arguing," I said. "But I don't know what it is."

"That's because you don't know what *it* is," Eddie said. "Have you asked the girl? Seems to me that she'll know all about this mysterious *it* your demon pals are looking for."

My gut twisted, but I knew he was probably right. There was just too much coincidence. Eliza showing up right here, right now. Her being at the market, and then in the alley. Not to mention the demon attacking her by the station.

Did the demons think that she had the mysterious *it*? Or was there some larger piece of the puzzle that I was missing?

"Keep an eye on her," Eddie said. "But don't trust her."

"Don't worry," I said cannily. "It's not my first day on the job."

"No, it's not," he said. "But even a seasoned Hunter can get stupid. Don't get stupid, Kate. Stupid makes you dead. And I don't want to eat out of a microwave for the rest of my days. Your cooking may not be great, but it's a step up."

"Thanks so much." I sprawled on the bed, my mind whirling. "Maybe Debbie learned something before she died. Maybe my parents gave me something or told me something. Maybe she told Eliza and a nurse overheard, and the demons found out, and—"

"You're stretching," Eddie said as I stifled a huge yawn.

"I know," I admitted. "Tell Laura to check out Duvall, okay? And if there's anything you can do—"

"What do I look like? Your minion?"

"You're supposed to be my *alimentatore*," I said archly. He'd taken over the role of mentor/trainer recently, and while I was pleased with the way it was going, we were both still getting our feet wet in the dealing-with-each-other department.

"Thought I'd get a few days of peace when you bounded off to Rome," he grumbled. "But yeah, yeah, I'll think on it for you."

"How very generous of you."

"Any other crises? Because my popcorn's getting stale."

"Enjoy," I said, then closed my eyes as I clicked off.

Just a minute, I thought. Just one short minute to relax, gather my thoughts, and then I'd—

"*Mommamommamomma!*"

I sat bolt upright, which was a mistake, as my head started to spin. I was under a blanket and the sun was streaming in through the window, cutting swaths of light and dark across the room.

Timmy was bouncing on the bed, reaching into and out of the light, and giggling like crazy whenever his hand illuminated.

I shifted, blinking, then peered at my husband, who stood in the doorway wearing jeans and a white souvenir T-shirt with the Italian flag emblazoned on it. I scooted backward to lean against the headboard. "When did you get that?"

"Last night," he said. "I took the girls out. I scored many brownie points by shopping with not one but two teenagers."

"Last night," I repeated stupidly. "You mean I—"

"Had a really excellent night's sleep," he said.

"Oh. Wow." I frowned at him. "You should have woken me."

"No," he said, grabbing Timmy around the waist and holding him upside down. "You needed it."

He plunked a pile of boy onto the bed and then sat on the edge. Then he leaned in and gave me a kiss. "It's a brand new day," he said. "And after the one you had yesterday—and the one you'll probably have today—I think it's safe to say you needed all the rest you could get."

And about that, I had to agree.

CHAPTER 12

By the time I'd showered and dressed, I felt human enough to go downstairs. Once I had two of *Signora* Micari's spectacular cappuccinos and a giant bombolni, I was certain I could conquer Rome, if not the world.

Even Timmy was happy, picking at a jam-topped croissant and making a sticky mess that I repeatedly apologized for while the *Signora* repeatedly told me not to worry, that she was happy to both feed him and watch him if I wanted to take my breakfast outside. I finally took her up on that, filled another cup of caffeinated heaven, then wandered into the garden area to find Stuart bent over a map of the city and the girls heading back inside.

"Did I break up the party?" I asked.

"It's already hot," Allie said. "We're going to go change into shorts. Stuart has us walking everywhere. I mean, why have taxis if no one is going to use them?"

"That's one of the universe's biggest questions," I said. I tapped my watch. "Ten minutes."

Both girls nodded agreement, then disappeared inside. I walked the rest of the way to the table Stuart had claimed, and he scooted over as I approached, then tapped his forefinger on the two-dimensional image of St. Peter's Basilica. "If we all go together, I can do the tourist thing with Timmy while the three of you go see Father Corletti," he said. "And if we follow this route," he added, tracing his finger along the map, "then we can actually work in shopping on the way. I'm pretty sure that will win me Father of the Year."

"You're definitely in the running," I said, as I leaned in close to study the map. "But can I make a suggestion?" I tapped my finger on the nearby *Castel Sant'Angelo.* "Here first. The Vatican after lunch."

He tilted his head to look at me more directly, then took a long sip of his coffee before saying anything. "Father Corletti not around this morning?"

"He probably is," I said. "But I'm sure he'll be there this afternoon, too. And I know you want to see it."

"I doubt one of the city's ancient sites will disappear if we don't do it first thing."

"You never know," I said with a smirk. "But seriously, yesterday was definitely not all about Stuart. Consider it your reward for taking two girls shopping. Besides," I added, after I took the last sip of my own cappuccino, "I should spend some time getting a feel for Eliza before I introduce her to Father Corletti."

Stuart cocked his head. "What's wrong?" he asked, his voice lowered.

"Nothing," I said. "But I talked to Eddie last night. He reminded me to be smart. I figure I can only be smart if I'm prepared. And honestly, I love the *Castel Sant'Angelo*. I can't think of a better way to officially start our vacation than to go there first."

"Marriage," Stuart said dryly. "It's all about the compromise."

"I'm glad you realize that." I pushed back from the table. "Because you get to be in charge of the stroller."

"Lucky me," he said, then stood up as well. "What about Eric? He have anything insightful to add?"

"No answer," I said. "I'll talk to him when I can." I spoke lightly and hoped that Stuart couldn't pick up the worry in my voice. Just in case, I rushed on. "I couldn't get Laura either. Apparently she and Cutter had a hot date."

"Well, that figures."

I frowned. "Huh?"

"We leave town and miss all the hot gossip."

"Better than being the hot gossip," I said, then immediately regretted my words. "Sorry, I didn't mean—"

"No, it's okay. I imagine we *were* the hot topic of conversation for a while." He took my hand. "And I'm truly sorry about that. Maybe we should host a house party when we get back, just so the neighbors can see that we're a unit again?"

"And here I thought you loved me," I countered, making Stuart laugh. Because he knows damn well I'd rather be tortured by demons than play hostess.

We found the girls in the foyer with Mrs. Micari who, from what I heard as we approached, was telling them where to find the best shopping off the beaten tourist track.

"Can we go, Mom? The *signora* says the market has all sorts of stuff. It sounds kind of like the Rose Bowl Flea Market. It could be so cool."

"You are familiar with it, no?" Mrs. Micari said to me after she rattled off directions.

I shook my head. "No, but it's on the way. I don't see why we couldn't swing through." I needed to get gifts for Laura and Eddie and some of the neighbors, too. A street fair style market sounded like as good a place to start as any.

"You will very much enjoy, I think," Mrs. Micari said, beaming at the girls.

Signor Tagelli, the old man who'd been in the sitting room the previous day, paused on his way to the stairs. He looked at the girls, then at me. Then he turned to Mrs. Micari.

He didn't say a word, but her smile seemed to falter, and for just a moment I wondered if I'd misread the situation. I'd assumed he was either a guest of the B&B or a regular who came in for breakfast or lunch. Now I wondered if there wasn't something more intimate going on. Because right then I was feeling the kind of tension that didn't tend to pop up between casual strangers.

Then again, if Mrs. Micari was having a torrid affair—or even a tame one—that was hardly my business.

Stuart had broken off from me to run upstairs for the diaper bag and umbrella stroller, and now he came back down. My thoughts shifted from the soap opera of Mrs. Micari and the *signor* to the more practical question of how to keep my troupe together as we braved the wilds of Rome.

Mostly, I just decided to wing it.

I told myself I wasn't being lazy. Instead, I wanted to watch Eliza. To get a feel for her without a formal interrogation. All true. But mostly I just wanted to slide drama-free throughout the day.

It was a lot to hope for, I know, but I am nothing if not optimistic.

Outside, the sun was shining brightly. The old buildings gave the entire area a look of appealing charm, and the shiny cars and bicycles added a bright glow that only underscored the overall feeling that on a day like this, nothing could possibly go wrong.

"Oh, man, Mom! Do you smell that?"

How could I not? The yeasty, sugary scent that came from a bakery just down the street was enough to make my mouth water despite the fact that I was still full from breakfast.

"Can we? Can we please?"

I looked at her, then at Eliza, who didn't beg with words but managed a puppy dog look that seemed achingly familiar. "Fine," I said. "We'll just eat our way through Rome."

The girls high-fived each other, then took off that direction. Stuart and I strolled more leisurely, as I was determined not to chow down on another carb-filled pastry.

That plan was all shot to hell when the girls emerged with cupcakes. After all, there's only so much temptation a woman can take, and when it comes to sugar, I'm as weak as they come.

I'm also weak where it comes to jewelry, because over the next two hours I bought two pairs of earrings and a matching silver and leather bracelet from a street vendor in the market. That, however, was nothing compared to the girls. In less than two hours, they managed to buy five T-shirts, four necklaces, two purses, one backpack, three retro-style metal placards with an Italian flag, three chocolate bars, and a wooden yoyo. The last was for Timmy and scored Allie a few points on the good sister tally card.

Stuart didn't do too badly either, managing to haggle forty American dollars off the cost of a gorgeous leather briefcase.

On the whole, it was a lovely morning, all the more so because it seemed so incredibly average. We all got along, and even the small talk with Eliza was comfortable. She knew a little Italian, which she told me was from high school and not any connection to *Forza*. She told stories about San Diego and enticed Allie with the possibility of learning to scuba dive.

Allie told about her pre-Hunter training stint at cheerleading, about her best friend Mindy, and about the fact that she was getting her drivers' license soon. The latter was said with a significant glance my direction, which I chose to ignore.

Even Timmy was an angel, alternating between singing to himself, chewing on the yoyo, or begging Stuart for another knock-knock joke. I'd been nervous about taking him out without Boo Bear, but so far he was doing just fine. And I didn't have to keep constant vigil against the horrors of a lost lovey.

The day was going so well, in fact, that when we sat down for lunch I almost suggested blowing off *Forza* altogether. Frankly, a day without demons was such a rarity that even if it meant waiting another twenty-four hours to see Father Corletti, I was sorely tempted.

That, however, was not the way responsible Demon Hunters behaved. And like it or not, Responsible Demon Hunter was as much my title these days as Mom.

"So are we all shopped out?" I asked as we parked ourselves at one of the pretty little fountains in a small cobble-stoned square. Despite stuffing ourselves that morning—and the fact that it was barely noon—we were all starving. We'd bought sandwiches, light salads and cookies from a vendor and now Stuart was passing the wares out to everyone. I was perched on the edge of the fountain with the girls sitting on the warm stones in front of us. Stuart was standing, and Timmy was the real royalty—the only one with his very own throne.

"You were here two days before us?" I asked Eliza. "What did you do?"

"I—" She started to answer, then stopped, her brow furrowing as she looked over my shoulder.

I started to turn, but when I heard Allie gasp, my slow movement shifted into high gear. I was on my feet and looking past the spray of water within seconds.

"The demon lady," Allie whispered. The commentary was unnecessary, though. I knew the woman well. After all, I'd seen her twice before—at the market where she'd threatened to kill my son if I didn't protect the mysterious *it*. And again at the subway when she'd tried to kill Eliza.

She was staring straight at Eliza. Then she turned deliberately to me before snapping her attention away, turning sharply, and heading into the throng.

"Stay here," I said to the others.

"Mom!" Allie protested.

"Kate!" Stuart and Eliza chimed in at the same time.

"I mean it," I yelled over my shoulder as I set off after the woman, trusting Stuart to keep Allie in line. And, hopefully, Eliza, too.

Unfortunately, the demon had a head start on me, and I lost her in the crowd. I cursed aloud, and was making a slow turn to scope out the area, when the sharp ring of my cell phone startled me.

I snatched it out of my purse, saw that it was from Laura, and took the call. My demon search could wait. Right then, I had best friend drama to attend to. "A hot date?" I said, right off the bat. I kept turning, my gaze skimming over every face in the crowd, but I couldn't escape the sinking feeling that I'd lost the opportunity to catch her.

"Hot as sin," Laura said on a sigh. "Can I just say that Sean is in about a billion times better shape than Paul ever was? I mean, the man had love handles even back when we first started dating. Sean's solid muscle, but I promise you, there's still enough love to handle."

She chuckled at her own joke, and I forced myself to sound stern instead of amused. "I think we've just crossed into over-sharing," I said. "That's my trainer you're talking about."

"Oh, please. Like you don't know he's hot."

She had a point. "Since when did you start calling him Sean?"

Laura, however, declined to answer. Instead, she just hummed a little, and that time I did laugh out loud.

"Sounds like things are going well at your end, too," she said. "Even with the whole dead demon in the airport thing."

"So you got my message?"

"Sorry it sat in my voice mail for so long. It's been a long time since anyone took me away for a romantic weekend. And considering you're about three thousand miles away I didn't expect to be called into research mode."

"You're totally forgiven," I said. "But if you can take a break from living out your sexual fantasies for a few hours, I really could use the help."

"Already on it," she said. "Duvall came from money, and that's making it easier. Apparently he was one of the pretty boy trust fund types. The kind that dates celebrities and gets into trouble. Lots of articles in the paper over the years about various run-ins with the law and stuff like that. Then he seems to have gotten serious about school— probably told by Daddy that if he didn't shape up he'd get cut loose."

"Sounds like it," I said.

"Then he was a in a car accident about two months ago. Nasty one. The kind no one walks away from, but he did. You know the drill."

"I do indeed," I said, and as I spoke my friendly neighborhood demon cut diagonally in front of me. She walked in firm, determined steps. And I—equally determined—set out after her. "Go on," I said, but now my voice had dropped to a whisper.

"What's going on?" Laura said, obviously cluing in to my change of tone.

I gave her the quick and dirty run-down. My demonic encounters. My familial encounters. The whole shebang reduced to quick soundbites given on the fly. Fortunately Laura and I knew each other well enough that she could interpret both the words and the emotion.

"Jesus, Kate, you must be ripped up."

"Something like that," I agreed. I paused beside a stall selling roasted nuts and watched as my quarry lingered outside a store front.

"She's really your cousin?"

"I think so. And I think I trust her. But—"

"But you trust Eric more and he told you not to trust anyone."

"You got it."

"I'm with Eric. Watch your back, Kate. I'm worried for you. I wish we could have come, too," she said. "Finances are just too tight."

"I know," I said. "And it's hardly a dream vacation if I'm spending the days chasing demons."

"I want to help."

"You can. Find me some answers." My quarry started to move again. "Listen, I have to go."

"Wait—"

But I didn't wait. The dark-haired demon had turned abruptly to her left and then disappeared down a narrow alley. Since I wasn't about to lose her again, I followed, retrieving my stiletto from my purse as I did. I got a few questioning looks—most tourists don't walk around armed—but no one tried to stop me. Neither did they follow me, and I entered the alley alone.

The stench hit me straight off. The sickly sweet smell of rotten fruit combined with moldy meat and other not-so-delectable delicacies.

I gagged, took a step back, and was immediately shoved forward by the press of two firm hands against my ass.

I fell forward, landing hard on my knees and yowling with pain even as my attacker thrust down against my shoulder blades. I exhaled with an *oof*, then froze as I felt the press of a hand at the back of my neck—and a knife blade.

I cursed myself. I'd been so busy chasing after the woman that I'd completely ignored the possibility that she wasn't working alone.

My mind whirled with possibilities, but unfortunately, none ensured that I'd get out of this mess without my jugular being sliced open.

I was about to go for it anyway—thrust my head sharply back and try to whip around before he could reposition the knife—when I heard a high-pitched *whizz* and felt a whoosh of air brush against my cheek and ruffle my hair.

Almost simultaneously, the pressure on my neck decreased, and then the knife clattered to the ground. I stayed frozen for a moment—too baffled to move—then I looked up.

The dark-haired demon from the market stood with her feet planted in front of me, her expression stern.

And right there behind me was the body of the demon who'd attacked me—the child-sized body of the demon who'd first stolen Allie's backpack, and who had presumably ransacked our room. And who now had a knife protruding from his eye.

CHAPTER 13

"Don't even think about moving," I said as I climbed to my feet. I had the child-demon's knife in one hand and my own stiletto tight in my other.

The dark-haired demon stood straight, her feet slightly apart, her hands at her sides. "I am unarmed, you see. And now is the time to talk."

"Talk?" I repeated. "What the hell do I need to talk to you about?"

"The key," she said. "You must—"

But she didn't finish. Her words—and her corporeal life—were cut short by the knife that zinged through the air to land dead-on in her eye.

It all happened in a split second. The silver blade. The shimmer of the demon as its essence escaped the body. And then the thud of feet approaching from behind.

I turned, armed and ready, as Eliza rushed forward, followed by Allie and Stuart, with Timmy clutched tight in his arms.

"Jesus, Kate!" Stuart called.

"Out," I said. "We need to get out of here now."

So far no one else had wandered into this dark and smelly alley. But I really didn't want to get rousted by the Italian police. *Forza* used to have people placed within the various local law enforcement offices, and I had no reason to doubt that was still true. Even so, I hardly needed the hassle.

Instead, I hurried everyone out of the alley, through the market, and down a side street. When we'd reached yet another fountain in yet another square, I gathered everyone close, sat down, and took my first deep breath.

"Kate," Stuart said, and there was no mistaking the urgency in his voice. "Are you okay?"

"That demon . . . " Eliza's words trailed off as she shook her head. "God, between the two of them, you almost—"

"No." I shook my head. "No, I don't think so."

Allie's brow furrowed. "What do you mean?"

"She killed the little kid demon. And then she said something about needing to talk to me. About the key," I added.

"Oh," Allie said, nodding with understanding.

"The key?" Stuart said. "What key?"

"Wait," Eliza said. "You're saying she killed another demon? Why would she do that? And does that mean that I screwed up? I mean, I didn't know. She's a demon, right? And she tried to kill me before. And she was right there in front of you and there were knives and a fight, and—"

I held up a hand to ward off her rising hysteria. "You did exactly right," I said. "Except for the fact that I told all of you to stay put," I added, giving them each my Stern Mommy look in turn.

"Kate," Stuart said. "You were attacked. I think it's damn lucky Eliza was there."

I agreed—though I couldn't deny that I wish she'd come fifteen or twenty seconds later. Whatever that demon wanted with me, she had information on this mysterious *it* that every demon in town seemed to think I had.

Then again, at least I now knew that it was a key. That much she'd managed to tell me before Eliza dropped her.

Eliza.

I turned my attention to her, shifting from Hunter to Mom when I saw how dejected she looked. She might legally be an adult, but eighteen was only three years older than Allie, and the young woman I saw still had the glow of youth— and the haunted eyes of someone who had recently lost a parent.

"You did great," I told her again, keeping my voice level and soothing and extremely parental. "Thank you for watching my back."

I watched as she swallowed, then smiled up at me. Her eyes shone with unshed tears. "Thanks." She scrubbed the heels of her hands over her face. "I'm really glad I found you," she said. She shifted, so that she looked at Stuart and Allie, then reached down for Timmy, who shoved his chocolate-covered hand into hers. "All of you."

"We are, too," I said, because this wasn't the moment to lecture whichever member of the family had decided that it was a good idea to feed the toddler chocolate. And then—because I thought she needed it and I knew damn sure that I did—I pulled her in for a hug.

She squeezed back, whispered a soft, "I'm sorry," then pulled away.

"Nothing to be sorry about," I said, but she just looked at the ground and shrugged.

I wasn't going to press the point. I'd learned a thing or two about dealing with teens over the last few years. Instead, I knelt beside Timmy. "Let me clean him up before he smears chocolate all over the stroller and we attract every ant and fly in the area."

I found the plastic case of baby wipes at the bottom of the diaper bag, then proceeded to clean up my little boy, who was starting to make cranky noises. I said a silent prayer in the general direction of St. Peter's and hoped that we'd make it through one more day with above-average toddler behavior. After all, so far he really had been an angel.

Maybe the holiness of the city was rubbing off.

As soon as he was as clean and shiny as could be expected, I pulled out a few more wipes and used those to doctor my hands. They were raw from where I'd fallen on the rough and filthy street, and I winced as I rubbed them.

Stuart's hand closed over my shoulder. "It could have been a lot worse."

I nodded. He was right.

I sat back on my heels. "I hate to do this, but I need to change our plans. I need to go in to *Forza* now. I need to see if Father Corletti has a clue about what's going on." I shot a look in the general direction of the alley. "And I need to get someone out here to take care of that."

"I know," he said. "It's okay. Demonic mysteries and potential apocalyptic moments first. Sightseeing once we keep the world from ending."

"The apocalypse?" Allie said, her voice rising to a squeak. "Who said anything about the end of the world?"

"Stuart's being funny," I said, then scowled at my husband. "Or trying to."

He shrugged. "Let's hope it's just a joke. But when a demon mentions a key, I think *to hell*. Or am I wrong?"

He wasn't, of course. But instead of answering, I fished out my cell phone and gave Father Corletti a call.

"Ah, *mia cara*," he said after I explained the situation—including giving him a quick-and-dirty rundown of the various demon-related events since our arrival. "This is not what I had imagined for your first trip back in so many years."

"Wasn't on my ideal itinerary either," I admitted. "You'll send a disposal team?"

While I was more or less on my own in San Diablo as far as body disposal was concerned, I assumed that Rome was still a full-service operation. Thankfully, Father Corletti confirmed that was the case. He promised that he'd send a team right away—and that he looked forward to hearing all the details as soon as the family and I showed up at his office.

I looked at Stuart, who was frowning down at me.

"You *have* been busy," he said.

For a moment, I didn't understand the tightness in his voice. Then I remembered that I still hadn't brought him completely up to speed on the various demonic encounters.

"I'm sorry. Really. I was going to tell you everything last night. But then I got distracted by the fact that I passed out from exhaustion."

"I know. I do," he said, as if to ward off my protests. He dragged his fingers through his hair. "I told you before I understand, and I meant it. But that doesn't mean it's easy. It just means that I want us to get through it."

"Then let me tell you now," I said. "Let's go to *Forza*. You can meet Father Corletti. You can hear the whole story. You can see the dorms, see the training area. Then you and Tim can either do the tourist thing while I give the girls a more in-depth tour, or you can join us, too. Full disclosure," I said, my arms spread wide. "Really, Stuart. I'm tired of keeping secrets. It may take me a while to get used to not keeping them, but please believe me that I want to try."

"All right," he said, reaching out and stroking my cheek. "Let's go."

I took his hand and turned to get my bearings. When I did, I caught Allie's eye—and saw the hint of worry there. But whether it was because she didn't want to share all our secrets or because she was afraid of what would happen when all those secrets came out, I didn't know.

She had reason to be wary, though. Stuart might think that he wanted the truth—he might even think he could handle a pending apocalypse—but the god's honest truth was that I still wasn't sure he was ready.

And that, I knew, was going to become a problem.

"Wow," Allie said as we moved through the quiet, formal halls of the Vatican offices. "I mean, seriously, wow."

Beside her, Stuart and Eliza looked around with equal amounts of awe and wonder. As for me? Well, I was striding down these familiar halls with a certain amount of pride. I may not be able to keep a clean house, but I'd grown up around pure, undiluted beauty.

Of course, that wasn't entirely true. Most of my life had been lived in the training rooms and *Forza* dorms, which had a decidedly less opulent feel. Visits inside the actual halls and corridors of the Vatican had been rare, mostly because *Forza* was a secret arm of the Vatican. And that meant secret from both the general public and from most of the priests and Cardinals and staff that lived and worked in this holy place.

Today, though, I was coming as a friend of Father Corletti's, and we were given the full treatment, including being escorted by two fully uniformed members of the Swiss Guard.

"I'm guessing this isn't where you spent most of your time," Stuart said as the taller of the two guards showed us into Father Corletti's outer office.

"You'd guess right," I said. "I'll take you out through the dorm entrance. It's considerably less formal. So much so that you're lucky if the wall lights are functioning."

A giant wooden desk dominated the far side of the huge room, and from behind it a young man in a familiar priest's robe rose to greet us. "I'm Katherine Connor," I said. "My family and I have an appointment with Father Corletti."

He nodded. "Of course." He spoke in a distinctly British accent, and I was reminded that working as the secretary to a man in Father Corletti's position was a coveted position within the Church hierarchy. "I am Father Caleb. It is our pleasure to have you here today."

"Are you new?" I asked. "I spoke with Father Gregory on the phone several times, but it's been many months."

Father Caleb nodded. "He serves in the United States now, in the Archdiocese of Los Angeles."

"Oh," I said. Though San Diablo was over an hour away from Los Angeles, it still fell within the LA archdiocese. "I hadn't heard. I'll have to look him up when I get back home."

It was probably my imagination, but I thought that Father Caleb's eyes glittered with amusement. "I'm sure he would like that very much," he said. He turned his attention to Stuart, the girls, and Timmy. "Father Corletti has been looking forward to spending time with your family, too. Please," he added, gesturing toward the huge, heavy door that led into Father Corletti's office.

We followed him in and found that Father Corletti was already up and coming toward us. He seemed smaller than when I'd last seen him, as if his priest robes were just a little too big. His hair was white and soft, as if emulating a cartoon image of heaven. He moved a bit slower, too, and I couldn't seem to shake that stab of loss that cut prematurely through me. He was getting old, this man I loved. And even though his eyes were as bright and sharp as always, I knew that one day, possibly soon, I would lose him.

"The flesh has no choice but to get old," he said to me in Italian.

"You always knew what I was thinking," I answered, the words and language a bit heavy from lack of use.

"It is the circle of life, Katherine." He shifted just enough to glance at Timmy. "None of us escape it. We can only seek to extend it, protect it, and to leave it with dignity and faith intact." He took my hands, then looked me over, his expression one I was familiar with, as I wore it myself when I looked at my children. This was pride, and I was both humbled and honored that I had lived up to his expectations.

He pulled me close, hugged me tight, and then drew back so that he could peer at my family through his thick, round glasses. "But I have forgotten my manners," he said, now in English. "It is so good to see you. All of you," he added, smiling at Eliza. "Father Donnelly told me of the death of your mother. She is with God now, but of course that is an insufficient balm for those left behind. Especially when those grieving are so young."

"I'm doing okay," Eliza said, though at that moment she didn't look to be doing well at all. To my surprise—and to Eliza's—Father pulled her close and hugged her tight, the gesture setting off a flood of memories of all the times that Father had comforted me when I had been young and sad and lost.

I sighed, then leaned against Stuart, taking comfort in the simple way his arm curled tight around my shoulders.

Next, Father Corletti crouched on his knees so that he was eye level with Timmy. "Ah, the glow of youth. He has grown considerably since last I saw him. As have you," he added, rising again and drawing Allie in for a hug. Finally, he turned to Stuart. "I think it is you that I am the most pleased to see. It is good that the secrets that have lingered between you and Katherine have been swept away, no?"

"I think so," Stuart said. "I hope Kate does as well."

"She does," I said firmly.

"But come," Father Corletti said. "We will have tea, we will talk, and then we will visit your old home. And after that," he said as he turned to Allie with a mischievous gleam in his eye, "Well, perhaps after that we can let you have a taste of what it is like to train in the same manner as your mother did, so many years ago."

"That would be fab!" Allie said. "Eliza, too?"

"If she wishes."

"I'd love it," Eliza said, and she and Allie started talking excitedly among themselves as we headed out of Father's office to one of the formal sitting rooms.

For the first few minutes, the conversation was as formal and stilted as the room, but I couldn't stay reserved for long. I was too happy to be there, to see him again. And soon we were talking easily about San Diablo and our old adventures, as well as these new adventures that had transpired since we'd arrived in Rome.

Allie and Eliza had been sitting on one of the small settees discussing weapons, but as soon as I started to outline all that had happened since we landed in Rome, I realized that they'd quieted down. The better to eavesdrop, I presumed.

In fact, Timmy was the only one who didn't settle. Instead, he beat his spoon loudly against a tea cup and hummed along in time with the music he was making.

"Why don't I take him out?" Stuart asked. "We'll go explore Vatican City."

"You're sure?" I asked. Stuart still wasn't party to all of my various adventures since we'd arrived, and I'd fully intended to educate him and Father Corletti at the same time.

"Trust me," Stuart said, packing Tim back into the stroller. "It's for the best." He turned to Father Corletti. "We're here for over a week. I assume this won't be our last visit. I'd love to see where Kate spent her youth. Perhaps next time I can beg a private tour."

"I will show you around myself," Father Corletti said. "I'm sure we have much to talk about."

Stuart looked sideways at me. "I'm sure we do."

Father Corletti rang for an escort, and I kissed Stuart and Timmy goodbye before they headed out on their own adventure. Meanwhile, the girls and I stayed with Father, and I finished telling him about a few adventures of my own.

"And you?" Father asked Eliza once I'd brought him up to speed. "Have you been plagued by the demons as well?"

She shook her head. "Only that one time, by the subway. But Kate already told you about that."

"And the alley?" he asked. "Where you threw the canister and assisted Kate's escape? What were you doing there?"

She squirmed, then shrugged. "Following Kate," she said. "And then I followed Allie to the bathroom, and then I saw Kate and the demon and, well, tossing that can seemed like a good idea at the time."

"A very good idea," I agreed.

After another half hour or so of meandering conversation, it was clear the girls couldn't take it any longer. "Should we take them in through the trainee entrance?" Father Corletti asked me with a conspiratorial grin.

"Absolutely," I agreed, then watched in delight as Eliza and Allie started out excited and then shifted toward apprehension as Father and I took them outside, across St. Peter's Square, and all the way back into Rome proper.

"Um, Mom? You told me you trained inside Vatican City."

"And I did," I said. "Have faith and follow."

To her credit, she did, and Father Corletti and I led the girls to the small grocery store three blocks to the east. We entered, moved through the store to the back, and then passed through the walk-in freezer to enter the long, underground corridor that led all the way back to the Papal Palace. Or, rather, to the training center and dorms that were built well beneath that grand and famous residence.

"Seriously?" Allie asked, huffing a little as we walked along. "You guys walked this every day?"

"Hardly," I said. "Most days we stayed in the dorms. Or we took an interior staircase up to the roof if we were craving sun or sky. But if we had to go out or get back in, we were doomed to walk the corridor."

"I guess it was part of the training," Allie said. "I mean, talk about exercise. What is this, like eight miles or something?"

"Not even close," I said. "And see? We're here."

The combination code for entry had changed since my day, of course, and I stepped aside as Father Corletti keyed in the lock code for the heavy iron door that had guarded these tunnels for centuries.

Once inside, I paused and breathed deep. The air was stale, but there was an undercurrent of spice and musk, sweat and excitement. It was rich and thick and alive—and memories flooded over me.

"You liked it here," Eliza said, and I realized that I was smiling.

"I did. It was home." I nodded toward the corridors that fanned out in front of us. "The dorms aren't that interesting. Let's take a peek, then show them the gym area."

The dorms had once been monk cells, and each tiny room was filled with four cots. I was able to show Eliza and Allie my actual room, and I ran my fingers lightly over the etching in the stone where

Eric had taken the knife he'd given me and scratched KA and EC.

"Daddy?" Allie asked, peering at the shallow carving.

"Yes," I said, though I'm not sure how I got the word out past the tears that filled my throat.

"He broke the rules often, your father," Father Corletti said. "I think that knowing when and how to break the rules was part of why he was such an exceptional Hunter."

If the expression of pride and pleasure on Allie's face was any indication, he'd said exactly the right thing.

"Where are the Hunters?" I asked. Though young and in training, the girls who actually occupied this dorm were full-fledged, albeit new, Demon Hunters. Once they turned eighteen, they would have the choice of coming on staff and working with the new recruits, moving on to *alimentatore* training, or taking an assignment out in the big, bad world.

Eric and I had taken the last option, working first in Rome, then later in various locations around the globe before we retired and moved to California.

"A training operation," Father Corletti said. "One of our Hunters in Berlin found a vampire nest. Since that is both rare and an opportunity, we sent a dozen of our young Hunters in for the clean-out."

"Sweet," Allie said, and Eliza nodded in agreement.

Both girls were sitting on the empty cots, and both looked content and at home. It was disconcerting, actually, how comfortable Allie looked in that room, sitting in the very location where I used to sleep.

I thought of Cami, my friend and roommate who had been killed by a demon during an operation while we were still in training. I thought of all the risks I had taken—and, yes, I thought of the excitement and sense of both duty and honor. The feeling of being part of something bigger than myself.

I wanted that for Allie—that sense of purpose and identity. And yet I was terrified of the price she would have to pay. Even if she was never wounded, she would have scars. There would be losses and tears and horrible memories.

She'd reached a point where I could no longer kiss the boo-boos and make them better. The circle of life, as Father Corletti had said.

But in the world of demon hunting, that circle could be a scary place.

"Mom?"

It might have been my imagination, but I thought I heard understanding in her voice. I smiled at her, then at Eliza and at Father. "I'm fine," I said. "A little melancholy."

"Can we see where you trained?" Eliza asked, standing.

"Of course."

Father and I led the way through the dim corridors that were still lit by wall sconces. Once upon a time, the illumination had been provided by candles. Now we walked in the dim glow of low wattage incandescents. Even with such modern touches, though, the corridor was clearly ancient.

The walls were rough stone, having been dug out and fortified almost two thousand years before.

Behind us, the girls were quiet for a while, apparently taking it all in—the dorm rooms we passed, each like the one we had paused in; the dining hall with its long, wooden tables and benches polished smooth from so many bodies sliding across them; the Hunters' library, which Father pointed out, also noting that there was a secret passage from this small research area to the actual Vatican library.

Soon, though, we came to the long pathway that had no rooms or passages extending from it. This was simply one long, dim corridor, and it was one through which I had passed every day of my youth as I moved from my sleeping quarters to the cavernous training floor.

"We're descending," Allie said, and the comment impressed me because the downward slope of the floor was so minute that most people didn't realize that by the time they reached the training room they were standing a full three stories beneath the ground.

For a while the girls walked in silence, but as they realized that we wouldn't be reaching our destination quickly, they began to chatter. I was already deep into conversation with Father Corletti, running through various theories about why I'd been targeted by the local demon population—and what they thought that I had.

Even so, I couldn't help but smile when I overheard Allie tell Eliza that it was good that Timmy and Stuart left, because her brother would have "totally melted down by now, and without Boo Bear he'd be making us all miserable."

She might not know the answer to the overall demon question any more than I did. But about that one little fact, she was totally on target.

"Ah, Marcus, you are here," Father Corletti said as we stepped into the huge, open space in which I had spent so many hours. Across the room, a young man in sweats who'd been beating the crap out of a sparring bag turned to look at us.

"Father," he said, "good to see you."

"Perhaps you could show these two young ladies a thing or two?"

"I would be honored," Marcus said, coming to us with his hand extended to me. "You are Katherine? I have been looking forward to meeting you. My father spoke most highly of you." He spoke in clear, slow English, and his smile was wide and welcoming.

"Marcus Giatti?" I asked, remembering the young son of my trainer, Leonardo Giatti.

"Si." His grin was wide. "I have grown into my father's shoes."

"You have," I said. "I'd be honored if you'd show the girls a thing or two."

As he took an excited Allie and Eliza out onto the mat, I sat with Father Corletti on a bench.

"I'd heard that Leonardo was killed during a demon raid," I said softly. "I didn't realize that Marcus had stepped in to take his place."

"He is one of the best trainers we have ever had," Father said. "Though the loss of his father hit us hard."

I nodded, thinking again about what Father Corletti said about life and loss.

"Children often surpass their parents," he continued. "From what I have seen of young Allie, she will turn out to be at least as exceptional as her mother and father."

"Now you're just playing on my parental pride."

He laughed. "Yes, but I also speak the truth. Katherine," he said, and the change in his tone had me shifting so that I was looking directly at him and not at Allie, who was working with Marcus on the form of her kick. "I am glad that you are letting her train."

"I am, too," I said, speaking slowly as I gathered my words. "I wasn't certain at first—it's a scary world out there, even more so when you know what's in it. But it's important, too." My lips curved into a quick smile. "Most of all, I don't think I had a choice. It's in her blood."

"As it is in yours." He nodded toward Eliza. "We will speak more of the family history that you are starting to piece together. But now, while the girls are occupied, there is something I wish to discuss."

"Of course," I said, though I silently feared that something was horribly wrong.

"I wish for Allie to train formally," he said.

"Father . . . " I trailed off. We had broached this subject before, and both Stuart and I were adamant that Allie wasn't going to give up the rest of high school.

"No," he said. "You do not understand. I wish her to train formally in San Diablo. And it is my desire that you step in—again, formally—as her trainer."

CHAPTER 14

"You're serious?" I asked. Me? Training Demon Hunters? "I can barely get a decent dinner on the table," I said.

Father Corletti laughed. "Perhaps not, but I do not recall any demon being slayed by the timely presentation of meatloaf."

I frowned, but not because I hated the idea. No, my discomfiture came from the fact that I liked it a little too much.

From across the room, Eliza let out a loud whoop even as Allie went sprawling on the mat. Seconds later, my daughter sprang to her feet. I tensed, not sure what her reaction would be. But she bounced to Eliza, congratulated her on "kicking my ass majorly," and then asked the older girl to show her how she'd managed the maneuver.

She saw me looking and flashed me a quick, happy grin. "Can we just move here, Mom? I am so totally loving this."

"Roomies!" Eliza said, and they both laughed as they high-fived each other.

I tensed, thinking about my daughter halfway across the world, training without me. I could keep her in California for three more years. After that, the decision was hers to make.

But if there was a training facility right there at home . . .

Beside me, Father Corletti pressed his hand over mine. "We will not speak of it any more today. I ask only that you think about it, and do not discount the possibility outright."

"I won't," I heard myself saying. "I don't know if I could pull it off, but I promise you I'll think about it."

"Good," he said, then stood up and waved to the girls. "I am going to show Katherine my roses in the garden. You are welcome to join us, but you are also welcome to remain with Marcus. I believe he may be in the mood for weapons training."

Allie and Eliza exchanged glances, and then Allie waved at me, her smile impertinent. *"Ciao,* Mom," she said. "We're staying here."

"Color me completely unsurprised," I said as I followed Father Corletti out the rear exit. We walked in companionable silence until we emerged in the private garden that had been his favorite spot for as long as I could remember.

"It's lovely here," I said. "But I don't really believe that you wanted me to see the roses."

"Ah, but I do," he said. "I want us to look at beauty while we discuss the ugliness that plagues the world."

I sat on a small stone bench. "You know what it is that the demons think I have?"

"No," he said. "But I can make an educated guess."

"I'm listening."

"You are aware that the altar in San Diablo was vandalized recently?"

I nodded. "Eric told me."

"I believe that I know why." He paused, but I said nothing. After a moment, he stood. "Both the Old Testament and mythology refer to gates leading into hell. You are familiar with such lore, of course?"

"Um, sure." I frowned, not particularly liking where this was going. "Are you saying that San Diablo has one of those gates?"

"I am saying that the altar hid one of the keys."

"I—" I closed my mouth, unsure what I had intended to say. "Wait. Seriously? How do you know? And why wasn't I told?"

"The key was discovered many years ago during an archeological dig. The Vatican gave permission for it to be hidden in the altar. Only three people on this earth knew—myself, the Pope, and the Hunter who placed it within the altar. And I have only known this truth for the last twenty-four hours."

"Who was that Hunter?"

He sat beside me. "Your grandmother."

"Oh." I leaned back, not entirely sure how to process that information. "So that's why they think I have it. And probably why they've attacked Eliza, too. It makes sense that my grandmother's kids were told the truth, and with both my parents and Eliza's being dead, we're the only two with a connection."

"That is my theory, yes."

"But I don't know where it is. And if I don't, and Eliza doesn't, and these demons don't . . . well, then doesn't that mean that a key that can unlock a gate to hell is missing?"

"I'm afraid it does."

"This really isn't good."

He sighed and sat down next to me. "I will agree with you, *mia cara.* But I will also say that we rarely face a crisis that is good."

I couldn't help it. I laughed. "Fair enough."

It was my turn to stand, because I couldn't seem to wrap my mind around all the thoughts swimming around in my head.

"So someone desecrates the altar and takes the key. And the demons assume it's me because I'm the local Demon Hunter, and suddenly I'm winging my way to Rome."

"That is my theory, yes."

"All right. But who really has the key? And who killed Thomas Duvall?"

"I do not know, Kate. But these are questions we must answer."

I ran my fingers though my hair. "I'll call Eddie. He can go poke around at the cathedral, ask questions. I don't know. Maybe we'll get lucky."

"Naturally we have turned all our resources to the question as well. If there is even a hint of a whisper of a rumor, a *Forza* agent will hear about it."

I scowled. "That presumes that whoever took it will talk. If I'm the person looking to open the gates, I'm going to keep my mouth shut."

"I'm afraid you have a point. However, that also presumes the person knows how to utilize the key and where the gate is located. Both are big presumptions."

He had a good point. "So we focus on people— or demons posing as people—who are researching the location of the gates and this particular key."

He nodded. "I should also tell you that I spoke with Eric. He was unable to reach you and was concerned. As you and I had not yet spoken, I told him that all was well as far as I knew. But now . . . "

"I left him a message," I said. "I'll bring him up to speed when he calls."

"I apologize if I overstepped my bounds."

"No," I said stiffly, though I was unsure why I felt defensive. "No, he should know. And he is my partner. He's—he's had a lot to deal with, and I hate worrying him. Especially when he's so far away. But if he's in the loop, even for research, then . . . " I trailed off with a shrug.

"Then you have to tell Stuart or else feel as though you are keeping secrets that you should not be keeping."

"Pretty much," I admitted.

"Every path in life has its pitfalls and its joys, Katherine."

"Yeah," I said wryly. "And I've got marriage and demon hunting. High drama on both counts."

As I'd hoped, he laughed.

I moved to sit on the edge of a low fountain. I wanted to ask him about taking on the role of trainer. I wanted to bat around more ideas about this key. I wanted to just kick back and reminisce about the past.

Mostly, I just wanted to sit and think and let everything that had happened settle over me.

Instead, I got teenage drama.

"Mom!" Allie called, bursting into the garden with Marcus right behind her. "Is Eliza here? Marcus said he'd show us the Vatican library, but I can't find her."

"She was with you. What do you mean you can't find her?"

"She went to the bathroom, then said she was going to get something to eat."

"I showed her where the mess was," Marcus said. "I got her a cup of coffee and a pastry. But Allie wanted to work with the crossbow, so we left her. I assumed she went to explore the dorms, but we've been unable to find her." He turned his attention to Father Corletti. "I apologize, Father."

Father Corletti waved the words away. "She is not the first teenager to wish to explore the maze of *Forza* on her own, and she cannot go where she is unwelcome without a code for access. Come," he said, standing. "If we all look, we will find her more quickly. Undoubtedly in the last place we look," he added, with a wink to Allie.

I was following them back inside when my phone rang. "It's Laura," I called. "I'll catch up with you. Hey," I said, as soon as the call connected. "Guess where I am."

"Rome," she said. "Listen, I need to talk to you."

I shifted to work mode immediately. "Go."

"Okay, so I told you Duvall was a trust fund baby, right? That he hangs with celebrities and makes the news? Well, there was this arrest that hit the *Times* Entertainment section. About a month ago. That's after the car accident."

"After he was a demon," I said. "Interesting."

"Yeah, I thought so too. But it gets even weirder. The arrest was for assault. Apparently he tried to shove the heel of a woman's shoe through some guy's eye."

"One demon trying to kill another demon?"

"I told you. Weird, right?"

"Very," I agreed.

"Well, hold onto your socks, because it just gets stranger. The shoe belonged to a woman named Deborah. Deborah Michaels. Kate," Laura said, her voice dropping, "I'm pretty sure she's your aunt."

My mouth was suddenly very dry. "I don't know her last name," I admitted. "I didn't think to ask."

"There was a picture in the paper," Laura said. "Kate, she looks just like you. Somehow or other, your aunt was working with a demon. What the hell does that mean?"

I shook my head in silence. I didn't have a clue.

"But it doesn't make any sense," Allie protested. "Maybe it wasn't the accident that took Duvall out. Maybe he was still human when he and Deborah got arrested."

"Maybe," I said. "But I doubt it."

We were in a black Vatican-issued sedan, and the driver was speeding me, Allie and Father Corletti toward the B&B.

"You think that Debbie was working with Duvall? And that they decided to go all postal on a demon? Why?"

"I don't know," I said. "But odds are good it had something to do with the key."

"So, what?" Allie demanded. "A Demon Hunter and a demon worked together to steal the key? And then they both get killed? Or maybe they were working together to protect the key, and then they both got killed."

"Protect it?" I protested. "What? A warm fuzzy demon?" I glanced at Father Corletti.

"It is not likely," he said. "But there are demons who seek to earn their way back into God's good grace. I would not dismiss the possibility out of hand."

"Ha!" Allie said triumphantly.

"And we still don't know where the key is," I said.

"I think Eliza has it."

"Did she say something to make you think that?" I asked.

Allie shook her head. "No. We just talked about stupid stuff. What we'd done so far in Rome. She told me how weird it was not being able to travel with her knife in her boot. I really want a knife that slides into a boot, by the way."

"I'll get right on that."

"I told her she was lucky. She could have been traveling with her baby brother and the bouncing blue bear."

I laughed. "You told her about Boo Bear?"

"Are you kidding? That stupid bear was the floor show for most of the trip. She said she used to have a stuffed tiger. I don't think I had anything, did I?"

"You were fickle," I said. "A new lovey every week. But this is entirely off-topic. If she didn't say anything, why do you think she has the key?"

"Um, because there's nobody else on the suspect list?"

Not exactly sound logic considering we didn't even know who all the players were. Still, it was the only theory we had at the moment, and I was willing to run with it. "Let's assume you're right," I said. "If she has it, it needs to be protected. So why not give it to Father Corletti when we were right in the middle of the Vatican?"

Allie and I both looked to Father Corletti, but he merely held up his hands. "I do not have the answers you seek. Nor will we find them until we find the girl. But the fact that she has disappeared concerns me. Did she leave, or did she fall prey to bad dealings?"

"Inside *Forza*?"

"No organization is entirely safe," Father said. "And deception must root somewhere."

I sucked in a breath, thinking of what had been done to Eric by Father Donnelly and the Hunters he'd mentored. Supposedly Father Donnelly tried to pull them back when he realized that they were going too far, but that didn't change the fact that the seeds had already been planted and Eric suffered because of it.

If a demon-hunting organization could actually plant a demon inside one of its own, was it such a stretch to think that same organization might seek to control a key to hell?

"Shit," I whispered, then immediately cringed. "Sorry, Father."

He only chuckled.

I was about to apologize again, but my phone rang and I snatched it up, hoping for more information from Laura, only to see that it was Eddie. I answered the call. "You're on speaker with Allie and Father Corletti. Tell me what you've got for me."

"Gang's all there, eh? Well, you ain't going to like it."

I made a face. "There's a lot of that going around. Tell me."

"I got a friend who's got connections. Found your girl Eliza's plane reservation. Last name's Michaels, by the way."

"Laura found that out, too. How does that help me, Eddie? I already know she traveled here."

"Because she didn't come alone," he said. "Deborah Michaels was in the seat right beside her. And before you ask, I checked. The seat was filled, passport checked. The woman in 12C was Deborah Michaels."

"What about the car accident?"

"None I could find. No police record. No hospital record. No death certificate."

"What's it mean?" Allie said. "Why did Eliza tell us her mom died?"

"Ain't that the question of the day?" Eddie said as the car pulled to a stop in front of the B&B.

"Eddie, thank you. Really great work. We have to go, but I'll call you back." I clicked off, then met Father Corletti's worried eyes before following him and Allie out of the car.

I hurried to the front door, opened it, and felt my blood turn to ice when I heard the familiar, gut-wrenching cry of my little boy.

"Timmy!" Allie yelled from behind me. She sprinted past me and up the stairs, with me following just a few steps behind. We tumbled into the bedroom together, where I found a very flustered Stuart trying to console a wailing, red-faced Timmy—who was clutching a mutilated Boo Bear tight to his chest.

Beside them both, Mrs. Micari stood wringing her hands, her expression one of utter helplessness.

"Kate," Stuart said, his voice tight. "Who the hell—"

"Eliza," Allie said, her voice flat. She looked at me for confirmation.

"Eliza," I agreed. I drew in a breath and met Stuart's eyes. "It was hidden inside Boo Bear. Thomas Duvall hid it inside the bear."

"It?" Stuart repeated. "What the hell are you talking about?"

I glanced at Mrs. Micari, who looked at all our faces, then hurried toward the door. "I get my sewing kit, yes? I fix the bear up for the little boy."

I nodded, then went to take Timmy from Stuart. He clung to me, the bear pressed between his chest and mine, little bits of stuffing falling all around us.

Allie closed the door behind Mrs. Micari, then slid to the floor. Father Corletti stood beside her. And Stuart sank slowly down onto the bed. "I get the feeling we're running out of time," Stuart said. "Which makes me think that I'm not going to get the full story. Tell me what I need to know, then tell me what we need to do."

I started to answer, but Allie got there first. "Thomas Duvall hid the key that opens a gate to hell inside of Boo Bear. Eliza took it. We're pretty much staring at the apocalypse now." She tilted her head up to look at Father Corletti. "That's the bulk of it, right?"

He reached for her hand. "A very succinct presentation," he said. "And unfortunately very accurate."

For a moment, Stuart simply sat there with his mouth slightly open. "But—well—*why?*"

"I don't know," I admitted.

"Eliza wouldn't be trying to open the gate," Allie said. "She *wouldn't*," she repeated when I turned to look at her.

"I liked her, too, Al," I said. "But that doesn't make her honest or trustworthy. Maybe it just makes us gullible."

"No," she said. "I talked with her. I would have known."

"Nadia," I said, and the name made her scowl.

"That was different," she said, but some of the bluster had left her. Nadia Aiken had eased into our lives—and yet she hadn't been who she'd seemed. Allie and I had both gotten hurt then. That wasn't an experience I cared to repeat.

In front of me, Allie sighed, then climbed to her feet and sat on the bed. She reached out to take Timmy, whose wails had calmed to exhausted hiccups. I passed him to her, then watched as she clutched her little brother tight.

"I get what you're saying," Allie said. "But it is different. No matter what else, she really is family. And that has to count for something, right? I think she's in trouble," she added. "I think we need to help her."

"Actually, I agree," I admitted. "But all we know is that the trouble is of the Very Big variety—because, hey, when you toss a gate to hell into the mix, there really isn't any other kind of trouble. But other than that . . . well, we don't know what she's up to or where she's gone."

"The gate," Allie said. "I mean, duh."

I didn't think it was quite as *duh* as she did, but since I had no better suggestion, I glanced at Father Corletti. "Do we even know where this gate is?"

"There are many purported locations across the globe."

"There's one in Turkey," Stuart said. "I read about it in the paper a while back. Made me think of that movie. *The Exorcist.*"

"She can't possibly have gone to Turkey," I said.

"She didn't," Mrs. Micari said as she thrust open the door and stepped inside. "She went to the catacombs. And by now, I fear the gate is already sliding open."

CHAPTER 15

"What the hell are you talking about?" I snapped. "The catacombs? There's a gate to hell in the catacombs?"

"Please," Mrs. Micari said. "You come downstairs. We will sit and I will tell you."

"You'll tell me now," I said. "I don't have time for tea and conversation."

She turned helpless eyes toward Father Corletti. "Please, Father. There are things that must be said. I will be brief," she added, turning back to me. "But it is important you understand. Katherine, you trusted me once. Please do not doubt me now."

"I do doubt you," I told her. "Right now, I can count on one hand the people in this world I trust. But I agree that I need information, so I'll give you five minutes. I hope you can talk fast, *Signora.*"

She nodded, then briskly left the room. Allie followed, first passing the now-sleeping Timmy to Stuart. "Go on," Stuart said. "I'll put him in the playpen and meet you downstairs."

I nodded, then hurried to catch up. When I did, I was surprised to see that *Signor* Tagelli, the old man who seemed to be a fixture in the B&B's common areas, was seated beside Mrs. Micari.

"Talk," I said.

"Fool," *Signor* Tagelli said. "The time for talk is past. Do you wish to see this world made over into Tartarus?" he asked, referring to the deepest pit of hell. "The girl will open the gate, and your stint on this sorry world will be over."

His voice was as rough as his words, and while I was reeling under the force of them, Allie was managing a more practical response. She stood up, pulled a spritzer of holy water out of her bag, and got him square in the face.

Immediately, the old man began to yowl.

"I knew it!" Allie said at the same time that I cursed, then kicked out to knock his chair backwards. Mrs. Micari leaped to her feet, and Allie sprayed a good dose on her as well.

All that happened, though, was that our hostess got very wet.

Meanwhile, I had lunged forward as Tagelli fell backwards, and I straddled him now, the stiletto that I'd cleverly hooked through a belt loop on my blue jeans now poised right at his eye.

"Katherine, no!" *Signora* Micari cried. "He has been working to keep the gate locked. He and Thomas Duvall and our dear Deborah."

"Ha!" Allie cried. "I told you. Good demons. Or, you know, as good as demons can get."

I, however, didn't remove the knife. At least not until I looked at Father Corletti. For a moment, he did nothing more than look back at me. Then he seemed to deflate. "Step back, Katherine. Let him up and let us hear his story."

Tagelli ended up telling his story in transit to the catacombs, because demon or not, I agreed with him that there was no time to waste.

"It was your grandmother who found the key," he said to me. "And it was she who was charged with concealing it."

"In the altar in San Diablo?" Allie asked.

"Yes, although I did not know as much at the time."

"How did you find out?"

He sucked in air through this teeth, the sound like a hiss. When he spoke, his voice was like a snarl. I shivered, reminded that I was sharing a Vatican-owned car with a demon. Even for me—a woman who'd seen pretty much everything—that was a first.

"Do you know what it is like? Do you understand the depth of the pain that cuts through you when you move from a noncorporeal state into a human shell?"

I didn't. I had assumed, in fact, that the process was painless. Like slipping on a coat. I thought of Eric, who had fought so hard to come back to me— to Allie—when he had been trapped in the ether. He hadn't mentioned the pain. Had he not felt it? Or had he simply borne it in silence, one more horror that had settled on the shoulders of a man who'd endured far too much?

I said none of that to the demon, though, simply waited until he continued.

"It is a pain beyond reckoning," he said, "and yet we endure it. We seek it out. Such fragile, puny shells you have and yet we are willing to suffer in order to claim one for our own."

"Why?" Allie whispered.

He turned to her, his eyes cold, and she shrank back, clearly remembering that it was not a man she was speaking to—not even an ally. He was a demon, through and through. In that moment, perhaps, our goals were aligned, but that did not mean we were on the same side, and I saw in Allie's eyes that she understood that, too.

"Because once the transition is complete, this form provides unspeakable pleasure. This world is open to infinite possibility. There is no flesh in the ether," he said. "No form at all. No smooth leather," he added, stroking the back of the seat in front of us. "No food, no wine."

I continued to watch Allie's face. I had asked the demon how he found out about the key's hiding place, and he still hadn't answered. Not directly, anyway. But I could see the thread of the conversation. Allie's brow was furrowed, though, and I knew that she was struggling to catch up. "There is form in hell," I said. "But no pleasures."

His lip curled up in an expression that was both smile and sneer. "That is so. And some of us— perhaps even most of us—do not wish for a hell on earth. Eradication of the puny souls that fill your mortal shells—that would not trouble us. But eradication of the flesh? Of the substance? That is not what we seek."

"Domination, not violation," Allie said.

He met her eyes. And he nodded.

"You're horrible," she whispered, and the demon laughed.

"Perhaps so. And yet you do not destroy me. Because I know where the girl is, and you do not."

"The catacombs," Allie said.

He inclined his head in agreement. "Indeed." He looked at me. "Tell her how many catacombs weave through the earth beneath this ancient city."

"Too many," I told her. "It would take a miracle for us to find her in time, much less on our own."

Allie seemed to consider that, then nodded. "But you still haven't answered my mother's question."

"This key—it opens a gate, yes. But that gate is not a simple door through which those corporeal demons bound in hell can travel. Instead, it is a gate that holds back hell itself."

"I don't understand."

Throughout all of this, Mrs. Micari had sat silent. Now she spoke. "Child, the gate will allow hell to seep out. Like a plague upon the land. Like a slime that covers and destroys."

"Mom," Allie said, the word like a prayer. Then she reached out and grabbed my hand.

"We do not want that either," Tagelli said. "And so we have waited. And so we have watched." He looked at Mrs. Micari, who drew in a breath before speaking.

"I have known for many years that the key was found and then hidden or destroyed. I hoped it would never be found again, but I have paid attention. And, yes, I have acted as a liaison with the demons who would aid us in our quest to keep the gate closed."

She looked at Father Corletti as she spoke, her eyes pleading as if for forgiveness or understanding. His face, however, was unreadable. She licked her lips, then continued.

"Deborah was obsessed with two things—finding out what happened to her sister," she said, looking at me, "and making sure that the secret of the key remained safe."

"Her mother told her where it was hidden?" I asked.

"No. That was a secret your grandmother took to her grave. I do not know how the truth was discovered, but it was."

"So the black hat demons are the ones who messed up the altar?" Allie asked.

"Black hat demons?"

"You know. The bad guys. And he would be one of the white hat demons," she added, nodding toward Signor Tagelli.

"I see, but no. Deborah retrieved the key. Your grandmother had broken it in two and placed each piece in a different part of the altar. One was cemented into some mortar holding the marble together. The other was incorporated within the scrollwork. Disguised. Camouflaged."

"And Debbie got both pieces?" I asked.

"Yes. She kept half, and the other half was entrusted to one of your white hats," she said with a nod toward Allie.

"Thomas Duvall," I said with sudden understanding.

"Indeed. They were to travel separately to Rome so that the keys could—finally—be destroyed."

"The black hats were on to him, though. And so he decided to hide his part of the key with us," Allie said.

"So I believe," Mrs. Micari said.

"But why not just destroy them in San Diablo?" I asked. "For that matter, why didn't my grandmother destroy them?"

"I do not believe she knew how," Mrs. Micari said. "There is a ritual for destruction, lost until only recently. And a place where that ritual must occur—the same place that the key must be used to open the portal."

"At the gate you mean?"

"No." This time, it was Tagelli that spoke. "The ritual chamber is miles away from the portal."

"I don't understand," Allie said. "I thought we were going to the gate."

"We are going to the catacombs," Tagellis said. "Where the key is to be used or the ritual performed. Where the girl Eliza must be."

Allie shook her head. "But—"

Father Corletti put his hand on hers, then spoke for the first time since our ride began. "The ritual location exists in a duality. Either for the destruction of the key or the opening of the portal. If you obtain the key first—even one of the pieces—and perform the ritual of destruction, then that is the end. But if the black hat demons place the key in the lock, then the portal will begin to open. And that will be the end as well."

"Oh." Her voice was very small, and I was reminded of how terribly young she was to have seen all that she had seen.

"But the gate doesn't open at the ritual site?"

"No," Tagelli said. "The key operates one of the gates, but that gate could be anywhere. Once activated, hell will begin to leak out. Slowly at first, as the crack will be small. Then faster as the portal expands."

"But where?" Allie said.

"As I said, it could be anywhere. Here in Rome. Back in San Diablo. Moscow, Queensland, beneath one of the Pyramids of Giza. There is no way of knowing."

"But that means . . . " Allie trailed off, too horrified to say the rest.

It had to be said, though. Because we all needed to know what was at stake. I looked at each person in the car in turn, then drew a deep breath. "It means that if we fail right now, then this really is the end of our world."

CHAPTER 16

As it turned out, I did know these catacombs. I had come to this very chamber as a teenager on my first big mission. We'd been sent to stop a powerful demon, Abaddon, and though we had succeeded, the price had been high.

Abaddon had been using a secret chamber within the twisting, winding maze of catacombs that snaked beneath the ancient city. At the time, that chamber had been locked, and it had been a minor miracle that Eric and I had managed to get inside before we were attacked by a horde of approaching demons.

Now, though, that door stood open.

Frankly, I didn't consider that a good sign. As far as I was concerned, a demon about to perform a horrific, world-destroying ritual would want to lock the door. Just in case any overeager Demon Hunters were rushing to try to stop them.

"We go in fast," I said, "but watch your back. Who knows what we're going to find in there."

Beside me, Tagelli and Allie nodded. I had debated letting Allie come, but the truth was I needed her. Father Corletti and Mrs. Micari had stayed behind, the first because he was too old and had never worked in the field, and the second because I feared that she would be more hindrance than asset.

Father Corletti had pressed to come, but I'd held fast. If what Tagelli said was right, the gate opened slowly. If we failed, maybe there would still be time to close the portal. I didn't know. But I was certain that without Father Corletti on the outside, even that slim hope was dead.

"Don't worry about me," Allie said. "I'm ready."

"I know you are," I agreed, pushing down both pride and fear. Both emotions were useless to me now. And sentimentality could get us both killed.

We were on a thin ledge by the open door, but from this angle there was no way to see inside the ritual chamber. In front of us loomed a seemingly bottomless chasm, which meant that we had to hug the wall until we reached the opening.

The risk, of course, was that as each of us rounded that corner, a demon would emerge, give us a shove, and send us tumbling down into the chasm.

It was, unfortunately, a risk we had to take.

"You," I said, pointing to Tagelli. "You're on deck first. Then Allie, then I'll bring up the rear."

I wanted someone to draw fire before Allie entered, but I also wanted someone after her in case she got shoved toward the chasm. It was hardly a foolproof plan to keep her safe, but at the moment, it was the best I could come up with.

Thankfully, Tagelli didn't argue, and as Allie and I watched, he edged toward the opening, then burst into the room. At first I heard nothing, then the echo of a woman's scream followed by a thud.

"Shit," I said. I grabbed Allie's hand. "We go together." Right then I didn't care if that wasn't the safest way to enter a room. I needed to see what was in there before she burst through that doorway, and at the same time I couldn't leave her alone.

"Together," I repeated. "We rush in, then you break left and I break right. If anyone is targeting us, that may throw them off. I know this chamber," I added, "and there's a chasm on the far side that you need to avoid if you get that far across the room. And there are stone columns that can provide cover for us or can hide an attacker. So be careful."

She nodded, and we hurried forward. I mouthed out the count, and on three, we rounded the corner, then immediately shifted low and rolled in our assigned directions—and I didn't even have time to applaud my own cleverness before the knives were flying.

We had the advantage, though, and Allie had her own knife out and airborne even before I was up and steady on my feet.

A few yards away, a female demon I'd never seen before toppled to the ground, Allie's knife protruding from her eye.

I didn't waste time thinking about it—or even examining the room more closely. There was another demon—a child—sneering at us from beside the newly-dead demon. It had a crossbow aimed at Allie, who rolled sideways as the demon let his arrow fly.

I aimed, released my own knife, and watched as the blade buried itself in his temple.

Unfortunately, all that did was piss him off.

I hurried forward, hoping to both retrieve my knife and reposition it in his eye. That's when I saw Tagelli's body behind a large stone urn. I felt no regret. Yes, he'd helped us, but he was also a demon, and once the threat of an all-consuming hell was alleviated, I had no doubt that he would have eagerly killed me and Allie and any other human who crossed his path.

I did, however, have one more use for him. I dove toward his body even as the young demon took aim on me. His arrow flew and I hit the ground, landing on Tagelli's prone, dead form. I grappled for his hand, then pried the knife he still clutched from his fingers.

I was in an awkward position, but I had to make it work. I had no leverage anymore, and the kid had already reloaded and was ready to release a fresh arrow. I'd dodged once, but this time I was certain I was in his sights.

I had one chance, and as I let the knife fly, I prayed this would work, then sagged in relief when my blade sank deep into his eye, and his falling body disturbed the trajectory of his arrow so that it missed me by a good three feet.

I glanced around, but didn't see Allie, and a new burst of fear had me leaping to my feet. I was just about to call her name when I heard her sharp cry of, "Mom!"

I ran toward her voice, then found her standing next to Eliza, who was bound to a stone column, her ankles tied with a thick hemp rope, and her hands above her, similarly bound at her wrists.

"Oh, god, Mom, she's barely conscious."

Allie's words were unnecessary. I could see for myself what they'd done to the girl. Her wrists were slashed and she was bleeding slowly, the process taking longer because her wrists were above her head. Still effective, though, and if the puddle of blood on the ground was any indication, the poor girl had very little time left.

"Cut her down," I said, though the words weren't necessary, as Allie was already sawing at the ropes. "Then cut some strips from her shirt and bind her wrists."

I was hurrying toward them as I spoke, but also looking around. I saw no other demon, but did spot the bodies of four that I didn't recognize sprawled across the floor.

"Your kills?" I asked Allie.

"Two are," she said. "I guess Eliza got the others. Quiet," she said gently as Eliza stirred in her arms. "We've got you."

I helped her finish sawing the ropes free, then we got Eliza to the ground. As Allie cut strips off her shirt and started binding her wrists, I stroked the girl's cheek. Maybe she'd betrayed us and maybe she hadn't, but right then she was simply an injured girl edging uncomfortably close to death.

"Eliza, it's Kate. Can you hear me? Where's the key? What happened to the key?"

Her eyes fluttered open. "Kate? Sorry . . . so sorry." Her voice was thin, so weak I had to lean close to hear her. "Didn't mean . . . said they'd let her go if . . . and I didn't, couldn't . . . "

"Shhh. It's okay. You don't have to talk."

"Gotta," she said. "Was supposed to bring the key from San Diablo. Supposed to destroy the key." She sucked in air and seemed to gain a little strength. "But they took her. They tortured her. They got the key from her." Tears spilled from her eyes.

"Your mom?" Allie asked. She was standing now, looking around the room.

She nodded, just a tiny motion. "She had one half . . . other half was missing . . . they told me I had to find it. That if I found it, they'd let her live."

I rocked back on my heels and sighed. *Shit.* Of course she'd kept the secret. Of course she would try to save her mother. What child wouldn't?

"You realized where Duvall hid it," I said.

"Yes." Another tear escaped to cling to her lashes. "I thought—I thought we could fight them before they used it. I thought they'd let Mom go and we'd still have a chance. Stupid."

"Where are they now? Where's your mother?"

The tears flowed freely now, and her whole body trembled with grief. "Killed her. They killed her anyway," she said as fresh grief and anger flooded through me. "They made me watch as they sl-sl-sliced her throat. And then, and then they said they were going to make me die slowly, watching as the world ended. I'm sorry, I'm sorry, I'm so incredibly sorry . . . "

She relapsed into sobs, and I stood up, fury bursting from me with nowhere to go and no demon to pummel.

"Where?" I asked Eliza. "Tell me where the demon is—the one who has the key. Where is the lock to open the gate? Eliza, honey, you have to tell me. They killed your mother. Don't let them win. Help me stop them."

"I don't know," she said. "They were here. They were right here, and then they just disappeared."

Oh god, oh god.

The demons had the key. Any minute now they were going to use it. And I had absolutely no clue where they were or how I could stop them.

"Mom?" Allie asked. "What are we going to do?"

But I didn't have a chance to answer. Instead, a voice rang out, rising from below to fill the chamber. "Going to do? You're going to die, of course."

And then, as we watched, an eerie red light burst out of the chasm at the far side of the chamber. Shadows cut through the light, and I realized that something was rising up from below. "Get Eliza," I said, as all the walls around us began to glow red, as if they were on fire. "Get her, and get out of here."

"I'm not leaving you," she said.

"*Allie.*" But the rest of my words died in my throat when I saw the demon standing on the chunk of rock that was rising like a column bursting from the miles-deep chasm. And there, sprawled at his feet, lay my dead aunt.

I recognized the demon immediately. He'd almost killed me in an alley by the Spanish Steps. Would have, in fact, if Eliza hadn't thrown that canister.

"You tried," he said. "But you have failed." He indicated the glow of lights around him. "It is already done. The key has been used. The portal has been opened." He took his foot, then shoved at Debbie's body. "Even now, the glory of hell seeps into this weak and ugly world."

As Eliza screamed, her mother fell over the edge of the pillar, to plummet down, down, down, into what I could only assume was the depths of hell, now rising to consume us all.

"You can try to kill me," the demon said, "but there would really be no point. There is no stopping what has been set in motion. But I thank you very much for taking such good care of the key. And I thank your cousin for so diligently delivering it to us."

"You won't win," I said, though I feared the words were a lie.

"We already have," he said, and then he smiled slowly, stepped off the pillar, and followed Debbie's path into hell.

The moment he disappeared from sight, the walls started to shake, and the glow deepened.

"Shit!" I reached down and hauled Eliza to her feet. "Get her other arm," I said to Allie. "We have to get out of here."

The destruction began behind us, but it was so fast we were barely able to stay one step ahead of the floor that began to crumble into rubble beneath us. There was no way that we could move fast on the ledge outside the chamber—not while we were hauling Eliza—and I could only pray that the destruction was limited to this chamber. If it took out the whole catacomb, we'd never survive.

Then again, the gate had been opened. Even if we made it out of the catacombs alive, how much time would we have bought?

But that wasn't worth thinking about. Right then, we just needed to get out. And with Allie and me hauling my injured cousin, we sprinted toward the exit, finally leaping clear just as the last few inches of floor fell away beneath us.

We hugged the wall, balancing on the thin ledge and catching our breath as behind us, the chamber collapsed into rubble.

A fitting end, I thought. And a fitting beginning to the end of the world.

CHAPTER 17

Time was running out.

Somewhere in the world, the gate to hell had opened. I imagined a black slime bubbling out, like red hot lava that would destroy us all.

Because we had no time, Mrs. Micari, Allie and I returned to the B&B to regroup and research. Father Corletti kept Eliza with him and returned to the Vatican where she could be cared for by *Forza*'s amazing medical team while he rallied the troops and did research of his own.

We needed to know two things, of course. Where the gate was. And how to close it now that it was open. Both pieces of information were essential, and neither was useful without the other.

Unfortunately, we didn't even know if there *was* a way to close it. We were flying blind, and had no time.

I called Eddie from the car, so he was doing what he could from Los Angeles, with Laura and Cutter and even Mindy burning up the Internet as they tried to find a clue. But I didn't expect much.

I'd also called Stuart—and had been royally pissed when he hadn't answered the phone.

Mrs. Micari suggested that I call the B&B directly, but by that time we were only blocks away. As soon as the car slid to a halt, I climbed out and raced for the door. I threw it open, and then stopped dead, completely flabbergasted by what I saw.

"Daddy!" Allie yelled from behind me, then sprinted toward him and threw herself into his waiting arms.

Just the sight of Eric was enough to knock me off-kilter. It was astounding enough to see him here, in Rome, but even though I'd seen him several times since he'd lost his eye, I still hadn't gotten used to the way he looked with the black patch. Edgy and dangerous and just a little wild.

That, however, was only the surface stuff. What really blew me away was what I'd seen before Eric had stood up to embrace Allie—him and Stuart sitting at one of the small dining tables, both talking earnestly over cups of cappuccino.

Apparently the demon had been right—the end of the world was upon us.

"Why are you here?" I asked, then immediately followed that with, "Has Stuart brought you up to speed?"

"He has. We've been talking about what to do should the two of you return without having destroyed the key."

"I hope you came up with something," I said wryly. "In case you hadn't heard, the end is nigh." There's a reason gallows humor flows during moments of terror and despair; if nothing else it lets you feel just the tiniest bit in control of the situation.

"We haven't," Eric admitted as Stuart came to stand beside me. "But Father Donnelly is on his way. I hope he'll have some insight."

"Father Donnelly? Why?" I didn't bother to hide my disdain. Considering what he'd done to Eric, Father Donnelly was not on my favorite person list. And forgive me for being petty, but if the world was coming to an end, I didn't want to spend my last moments with the man.

"He's the one who told Eric to come," Stuart said.

"What? Why? He hasn't been in the loop at all."

"He has," Mrs. Micari said from behind me. I hadn't even realized she was standing there, but of course she'd been following the conversation. "He has been involved from the very beginning," she said, as we all turned to look at her. "He is, in fact, the one who told Debbie that the demons were aware of the key's hiding place. He knew that your grandmother had hidden it, and he instructed Debbie to work with Quiric—that was Duvall's demon name—to retrieve the key and bring it to Rome so that it could be destroyed."

"He knew how to destroy the key?"

"It was one of the many rituals he discovered in his studies, yes. But when Debbie and Quiric realized that the dark demons were aware they had the key, they decided to try a different tact. Father Donnelly told Quiric about your upcoming trip. And it was decided that Quiric would use you to smuggle the key."

I gaped at her.

"Why are you involved in all of this?" Eric asked.

"We grew up together. We have stayed in contact throughout the years. I worked with him when I served *Forza*. And I have helped him with many of his projects." She met Eric's eyes. "Many of them," she repeated, and I saw the muscle in his jaw tense.

"I see."

"It was you who ransacked my room," I said, my voice tight and harsh.

"No," she said. "It is clear that the black hats, as you call them, realized that Duvall passed the key to you. They searched. I had nothing to do with that. And young Eliza—when her mother was taken and she was forced to do the demons' dirty work—she did not come to me. She held her secrets well. It is possible that she helped the young demon access your room, but I do not know if that is so."

I took a moment to control my temper. "Fine," I said, wanting things back on track. "Donnelly wanted the key here. He wanted it destroyed. Good on him. But why does he want Eric here? Because, guess what? I don't trust the son-of-a-bitch."

"Katherine!" Mrs. Micari said. "He is a priest."

"He did harm to a child," I said, looking at Eric. "He injured a lot of lives."

"He had only the ultimate good as his goal. He wished to find a way to fight demonic power. To turn it back on itself."

"We're not arguing about this now," Stuart said. "Right now, all I really want to know is how to stop the end of the world. If this priest can help us, then I say we let him. We can debate whether he's a son-of-a-bitch after we survive the apocalypse. Okay?" he said, looking hard at me.

I raised a shoulder. "Sure. You're right. Does he think Eric can help? Is that why he called you?" I asked, facing my first husband. "Because you have some unique perspective on the way demons think?"

I hoped that was the case. I really did.

"He didn't say," Eric admitted. "For all I know, he thought I should be with my family when the end came."

"Daddy . . . " Allie chastised as she leaned closer to him.

"Fine. We start from scratch. You," I said, pointing to Allie. "On the laptop. Make a list of every location that pops up as a supposed gate to hell. Every one. We'll have Father Corletti rally the Hunters across the globe."

She nodded, then scurried upstairs to fetch our laptop.

"I'm glad you're here," I told him. "I'm glad she got to see her dad before—"

He met my eyes. "Don't even think that," he said. "We've stopped worse threats. We'll stop this one. We have a hell of a team," he added, then turned slightly so that Stuart was included in the conversation.

I looked between the two of them. "I'm going to regret possibly ruining a good thing, but what is up with you two? Is this some sort of bucket list thing? Make peace before the end?"

"I simply told Eric that I couldn't imagine going through everything that he's been through, and then having to top it off with seeing you with another man," Stuart said.

"And I told Stuart that I owed him my life—literally."

I frowned. Stuart may have saved Eric from the demon, but he'd almost killed him in the process. And cost him an eye. Still, if these two warring men in my life wanted to enter into a detente, I was hardly going to argue. "Great," I said. "Fine. So, I think that while Allie's burning up the Internet, we can—"

I didn't get to finish my sentence, because the door burst open and Father Donnelly strode in. Mrs. Micari hurried to his side. And, to my surprise, so did Stuart—who immediately lashed out and punched the priest in the face.

"Stuart!" Mrs. Micari said, but I have to confess that I just laughed.

Eric managed to stifle his own reaction, but I knew him well enough to see the mirth on his face.

"You must be Stuart," Father Donnelly said, as he rubbed his undoubtedly sore jaw.

"You put my family in danger," Stuart said. "That goddamn key in a child's toy? My son could have been killed. And my daughter just walked up to the mouth of hell. What kind of man are you?"

"One who is trying to push hell back where it belongs," Father Donnelly said. "One who understands that hard decisions must be made in order for evil to be banished to the dark, and for the dark to be locked away from the light."

"That's bullshit," Stuart said. "If you think—"

"*Stuart*." My sharp tone caught his attention. "I don't like it either. But he may be the only one who knows enough about this to help us end it." I looked Father Donnelly in the eye. "Can you?" I asked. "Or is Stuart right and we need to kick your sorry ass out of here so that the grownups can get to work?"

"It can be stopped. And yes," he said, looking directly at Eric. "I know what must be done."

CHAPTER 18

"There are, as you know, many supposed gates to hell," Father Donnelly said as we all sat around the table and listened to him. "There is no way that we can know which gate has been activated. No way to know for certain. But I have made an educated guess, and I believe that we are dealing with a gate to hell located beneath the Roman Forum."

"Why?" Allie asked simply. "If there are eight billion gates, why do you think it's that one? I mean, yay if you're right, because it's not that far from here. But personally I'd like to be a little more sure before we start chasing our tails and maybe wasting time."

I stifled the urge to applaud, and I could tell from Eric's expression that he felt the same. My little girl was growing up—and hopefully we'd save the world so she could keep going with that.

"You are correct to be wary," he said. "But I called the National Seismological Institute, and they have just registered activity localized to that area. Combined with what I'm about to tell you, I think that we can be confident that is where the gate is—and that it has indeed begun to open."

"What you're about to tell us?" I asked.

"Have you heard of the *Lacus Curtius*?"

We all shook our heads. All except my daughter, who nodded.

Father Donnelly's mouth curved into a tight smile. "Prize pupil. I hope she is formally training to join *Forza*?"

"Let's keep the world going, and we can talk about that later. Okay, Al. Tell us."

"I don't know a lot," she said, "but I just found it on the Internet when I was researching before Father Donnelly got here."

"So it's a gate to hell."

"It came up in the search, but nothing in the article said that it was. Just that it was this mysterious chasm. And it kept growing and growing until some dude named Curtius threw himself into the pit. And that stopped it."

"So the gate requires a sacrifice?" Stuart asked.

"I do not believe so," Father Donnelly said. "It is not common knowledge, but records I unearthed in the Vatican library reveal that Marcus Curtius was able to seal the chasm through a blood-letting. But once his blood worked such magic, he was reviled and tossed bodily into the closing chasm."

"Nice," Allie said. "Save the world, get punished for it."

"So this means that human blood will close it. One of us has to get close to the portal and, what? Smear it with blood?"

"There will be a center of power," Donnelly said. "There will be ancient drawings indicating hell. Eric will be familiar with them from his *alimentatore* training."

"All right. So that makes Eric useful."

"He is more than useful," Donnelly said. "He is essential."

"What do you mean?" Allie asked.

Donnelly looked at her. "Does she know what happened when her father was a child?"

"I know what you did to him," Allie said, lifting her chin. "You and his parents."

"But you do not know why," Father Donnelly said.

"You were trying to create a fighter with demonic instincts and strength."

"In part, yes. More than that, we were trying to prepare for this day."

"Eric is essential," Stuart murmured, repeating Father Donnelly's words. "Curtius was like Eric. That was how he knew what to do. How he knew that it had to be him."

I looked at Stuart with surprise and approval—and at Eric with shock. "Curtius was bound with a demon as well?"

"As Curtius lived before the birth of Christ, we cannot be certain of much. But documents within the Vatican indicate that he was so bound, yes. A hybrid."

"And since you wanted a hybrid in your arsenal, you created Eric," I said. "You bastard."

"There is always a price for good," he said.

"Are you going to be okay?" I asked Eric. "You've got a blind spot now . . ."

"I'll be fine," Eric said firmly. "I've been training—learning to compensate. And," he added wryly, "I seem to have a knack for defending that side."

"A benefit of his hybrid nature," Father Donnelly said with something like pride in his voice. Honestly, I wanted to smack him.

"Wouldn't that have left with the demon?" I asked.

The priest raised a shoulder. "There are mysteries, Kate. And some we shall never know."

"It doesn't matter," Eric said, pushing back from the table to stand. "The bottom line is that I'm going in, blind spot or not. If my blood will end it, then I'll end it." He met Father Donnelly's eyes. "Where exactly am I going?"

We stood in the dark outside the famous Roman Forum, watching as the tourists traipsed around taking pictures and posing and generally being unconcerned about the end of the world.

"You're going under," Father Donnelly said.

"Under?" I asked.

"In 2006, archeologists discovered a tomb beneath the forum. The Vatican participated in an expansion from that dig, and we discovered a necropolis beneath that tomb. Based on the etchings—and the fact that the center of this necropolis is directly under the Curtius chasm—I believe that is where the gate has begun to open."

"Will we be able to maneuver?" Allie asked. "I mean, hell is oozing out, right? It's going to be, like, what? Bile and grossness?"

"I don't know," Father Donnelly admitted.

"And you're not going to find out," Eric said. "You're staying up here with Father Donnelly and Stuart and Mrs. Micari."

"I'm coming," Stuart said.

"The hell you are," I retorted. "If something happens to me, I am not leaving Timmy without a parent." I glanced at the black sedan in which Timmy slept, watched over by one of *Forza*'s drivers. "And you know damn well you aren't field ready."

"Sorry, pal," Eric said. "She's right. You'd be a liability, not an asset."

Stuart didn't look happy, but to his credit, he didn't argue.

"*I* am an asset," Allie said. "And I'm coming."

"Alison Elizabeth Crowe," Eric said, "we are not having this argument."

"You're right," she said. "We're not." She took a step closer to him, then poked him in the chest. "You know what, Daddy? You left. Walked away. And you're back now, and that's awesome and all, but guess what? You don't get a say anymore. Mom does."

A muscle twitched in Eric's cheek and I tensed, afraid that his temper was about to boil over. To his credit, he pulled it back. "Your mother will say no," he said slowly. He looked at me. "Won't you?"

I thought of how much she'd grown up over the last few months. Of how hard she'd worked, how far she'd come. I thought of Father Corletti's belief that she was ready to train, and how much she had helped inside the catacombs. I thought, too, of the fact that this might well be the end, and we needed all the help we could get. And, petty though it might be, I thought of how much Eric had hurt me by leaving.

I looked at Allie, then turned to her father. "No," I said. "Her mother is going to let her come."

I held Eric's eyes, trying to silently convey to him that she was ready. That he needed to have faith in me and faith in our daughter. After a moment, he nodded. "Then let's get moving."

We put on the *Forza*-issued hunting vests—fully stocked with knives and holy water and all sorts of lovely gadgets and gizmos—and I said a silent thank you to Father Donnelly for bringing an official—and well-stocked—vehicle. Then we followed him away from the tourists to a construction site about two blocks away.

"The construction is a sham," he said, nodding to a ramshackle shed that looked to be the contractor's office. "The entrance to the necropolis is in there."

I looked him over—and realized for the first time that he had no vest and no weapons. "You're not coming?"

"I will if you need me, but I have no field training. I fear I would be a hindrance. But if you think that I would be a help, I will suit up."

"No," Eric said. "If this fails, you might be able to come up with an alternative plan. And, frankly, I'm not interested in watching Allie's back and yours."

"I can watch my own back, thank you," Allie said.

"She's ready, Eric," I said. "And she's older than we were when we started."

"We don't have time to argue about this," he said. "So we'll talk about it after we save the world." He looked at me and Allie in turn. "Deal?"

"Deal," we said in unison, then followed him into the shed. He had a penlight out, and he shined it around, finally landing on a trap door in the floor. Allie bent, then pulled it open. I peered in, following the beam of light along a ladder to a black pit of impenetrable darkness.

I bent down and maneuvered onto the ladder. "Ladies first," I whispered.

They both nodded, and I started down. I'd pulled my own penlight out and I held it in my teeth. The anorexic light was insufficient against the soupy darkness, and the ladder seemed never-ending. I swear we descended for hours until finally—*finally*—my feet touched solid ground. Or reasonably solid ground, anyway.

"It's . . . squishy," I said, then shifted the light so that it shone at my feet. Immediately, I gagged. "Oh, god. I think it's blood. I think it's congealed blood."

As soon as I said the words, I knew I was right. The scent wafted up from the ground, thick and coppery and cloying.

"Mom," Allie said as she stepped off the ladder beside me. Her voice was choked, and I was certain that she was fighting not to gag.

"Pull your collar up and breathe through your mouth," I said. "It'll help."

Eric stepped off next. "It's only going to get worse," he told Allie. "Can you handle it?"

She nodded, then yanked the collar down and breathed deep. "If you can, I can."

"All right then," he said. "Let's go."

We followed an ancient stone tunnel for at least three hundred yards. The air was stagnant and stifling. Blood rose up around our ankles. We slogged on in silence, and I didn't know about my daughter or Eric, but I was beginning to wonder if we were going to have to walk all the way to hell before we had the chance to stop this thing.

Then, just about the time I saw a red glow in the distance, I started to feel a breeze.

"Where is that coming from?" Allie whispered.

It was a good question, and one I didn't know the answer to until the birds swarmed—thousands upon thousands of squawking, screaming, fluttering crows, each with preternaturally wide wingspans, and each beating their wings around our heads, our bodies, our faces.

"Daddy!" Allie waved her knife in the air to no avail.

"Holy water!" Eric cried, spraying it out in front of him and creating a barrier between him and the birds.

Allie did the same, and I followed suit, and we pressed forward, fighting our way through the wall of crows that moved with us, kept at bay by the power of God and His holy water.

And then, as quickly as they had come, the birds vanished, each dive-bombing the floor and disappearing into the blood that was still rising around our ankles.

"Where did they go?" Allie asked, her voice a low whisper.

"Better not to ask questions you don't want the answer to," Eric said darkly.

"Look," I said. Before, the birds had been blocking our view. Now I could see that the corridor opened into a chamber. It was empty as far as I could tell, but with some sort of cylindrical stone in the center. The stone was covered with markings, and the blood seemed to be leaking from tap holes near the bottom.

"That has to be it," Eric said. "The center. The control."

"Where you need to be," I said. "Be careful. Can you read the markings?"

"I can't see them well enough."

"Hang on," Allie said. "I think there's—yeah, here." She'd been patting down her hunter's vest, and now she pulled out a pair of tiny binoculars and passed them to her father. "There's all sorts of cool stuff in this vest," she said. "We totally need these at home, Mom."

"First thing," I said. "We get out of here and California still exists, I'll personally oversee the vest creation."

I expected Allie to laugh. What she did instead was scream.

I didn't blame her. Like something out of a bad movie from the 1940s, a dozen animated skeletons were advancing upon us. "Their heads!" I called. "Slice off their heads!"

"They're protecting the pillar," Stuart said. "We need to clear them out before I can get to it."

"You're sure that's it?" I called back as I lashed out with my knife and sliced off the head of an attacking, grinning skeleton.

"I'm familiar with some of the marks," he said. "We can't see it, but there will be a crevice on top to collect the blood—*my blood,*" he said. "And then that blood drains into the stone and runs down those veins. See the pattern?"

"Kind of busy now," I shot back, as I lashed out at the two skeletons that were on me, a knife in each of my hands.

Eric moved in and thrust his stiletto through the eye socket of one, then ripped up sharply and pulled the skull right off the neck. With a flick of his arm, he sent it flying.

"Thanks," I said. "Just three more. Two," I amended as I watched Allie mow one down.

Eric and I each slew one of the remaining, and then we continued toward the pillar, Allie taking the lead.

"*Stop!*" Eric called, and both Allie and I froze.

"What?" I looked around. The skeletons were down. The crows were gone. There was absolutely nothing to fear in this chamber anymore—and I understood perfectly why that frightened him. Because you can't fight what you can't see, and that's what makes the hidden the most terrifying things of all.

"The ground," he said. "Look."

Allie and I looked, and I saw that just a few steps ahead of us the texture of the floor changed. The blood still flowed from the pillar, but it followed a series of what looked like grout lines along a geometric pattern of tiles that formed a hexagon around the pillar. Each tile was like a pristine island in a sea of blood, and each was etched with a symbol I didn't recognize.

"Do you know what it says?" I asked.

"A bit. It's ceremonial. A dance, I think. A ritual dance around the pillar. Or to the pillar, maybe."

"It'll be booby-trapped," Allie said. "Probably really nasty booby traps."

"I don't doubt it," I said. "But what makes you so certain?"

I expected her to tell me about some obscure fact from her research. Instead, she rolled her eyes, reminding me that no matter what the circumstances, some things never change. "Duh, Mom. *Raiders of the Lost Ark*? That whole thing at the beginning when he's trying to get the idol?"

I met Eric's eyes, and despite the fact that we were surrounded by hell, the humor I saw there warmed me. "That's our girl," he said.

"Yeah. She is."

Allie frowned. "So your blood goes down along the pillar, and then it makes some sort of magic, and *poof*, the whole thing stops?"

"That's what I think," Eric said. "And I also think it's time to test that theory."

"Be careful," I said. "Whatever dance you're seeing, you follow the footwork to the letter."

He nodded, examined the floor, and started to head toward the pillar. At the first step, the crows appeared again—but they didn't attack Eric. Instead, they launched themselves at Allie and me.

"Stay focused," I shouted to him. "We're fine."

Fine was a bit optimistic, but I didn't want him worried or distracted. I didn't want him falling. I'd seen *Raiders* and I didn't want to see him getting impaled.

"The next attack will be on him," Allie said. "It won't be as bad as what will happen if he steps on the wrong stone, but it'll be enough to try and trip him up. To *make* him step wrong, you know?"

"No," I said, "I don't know. How do you? Can you read the etchings? The pillar?"

She lifted a shoulder. "It's just what I'd do. If I was making up this trap."

I scowled. Great. My daughter, the evil genius.

"See," she said, as a dense fog began to build between our position and the tiled area. Soon, I couldn't even see Eric anymore. But I had seen enough to know what he was battling. Specters. Noncorporeal demons who writhed around him, their appearance like mist, their visages the kind of horrific masks that make audiences in horror movies scream.

"They can't touch you," I shouted to him. "Remember they're not corporeal. Just keep moving—and stay on the right tiles!"

I heard no answer, and I met Allie's eyes. "Sound barrier?"

"I would, wouldn't you?"

I scowled, but I had to agree.

That meant that all we could do was wait.

And wait.

"I'm going in," I said when at least five minutes had passed. "I can remember where he stepped. This is taking too long."

"*No*." She grabbed my arm as I stepped toward the fog. "For one, it'll be poison, you know it will. And for another, you can't help him. It has to be his blood, right? So he has to make it there."

And then, as if the chamber understood us, the fog lifted and my heart soared when I saw Eric standing right there by the pillar, his knife held over the soft flesh at the base of his thumb. I saw the flick of the knife, saw him wince, and then I saw him squeeze his hand over the top of the pillar.

For a moment, nothing happened. Then I saw the veins fill with red. Faster and faster the blood flowed, finally reaching the base of the pillar.

I expected the taps to close, the blood to stop flowing. I expected, I don't know, angels singing. Trumpets announcing the triumph over hell.

Instead, a blood red light burst out of the top of the pillar and the blood began to flow faster.

"Eric!" I cried.

"It's not me," he said. "Goddammit, Kate! The wrong blood just brings the end faster! God*dammit*." He waved his arms. "Go! Get to the exit! It's ramping up. We're going to have a hell of a time getting clear before the blood rises and sucks us under. Go, dammit, go!"

"Go where?" I asked. "The world is ending."

"Father Donnelly. Father Corletti. They'll figure something out."

"How?" Allie asked as a tear snaked from her eye.

I grabbed her shoulders and shook her. "Don't you dare, Alison Crowe. Don't you dare go soft on me now. We have a job and we are damn well going to do it. You're my daughter, dammit. You're Eric's daughter. You're a Hunter through and through, and you are going to act like one. Do you hear me?"

She nodded, but she said nothing.

"I said, do you hear me?"

Eric skidded to a stop beside me, and Allie tilted her head up to look at him.

"Your daughter," she said slowly, and then her eyes grew wide. "Mom!" she cried, even as she grabbed hold of Eric's arm.

"Dammit, Allie," Eric said. "We have to go."

"*No!*" The word was fierce. Determined. "What if Curtius wasn't a hybrid? The documents are old, right?" She looked between me and her father. "What if he was descended from a demon? Not bound, but *of* the demon? I mean, what if a demon was in his blood?"

"So what?" I said. "That still doesn't help us because—"

But I couldn't finish the sentence. I couldn't, because I knew what she was thinking. And God help me, I feared that she was right.

"It'll work," she said, and before Eric or I could stop her, Allie had taken off running for the pillar—only she wasn't bothering about the dance.

Arrows flew at her. Crows swooped for her. Serpents rose from the lines of blood snaking between the tiles and coiled around her ankles.

She dodged everything. Killed any creature that got in her path.

And she made it to the pillar unscathed.

"Dear god," Eric murmured, his voice so low I barely caught it. "Father Donnelly did it."

"It wasn't you who was the experiment," I said, my voice thick with tears that I was determined not to shed. "It was your child."

And as we watched, our little girl—our sweet, innocent teenager with the demonic lineage—

sliced her palm and then slapped her bloody hand down on the top of the ceremonial pillar.

Immediately, golden light burst from the column, then flashed out and illuminated the room, vaporizing everything demonic that remained, from the skeleton remnants to the blood, to the final bits of mist. The flow of blood from the pillar ceased.

Most importantly, the pillar itself started its slow descent back into the ground.

We'd won.

But as I looked at my daughter and her confused, tear-streaked face, I knew that we had lost, too.

I just hoped we hadn't lost everything.

Allie sat in the back of the *Forza* sedan, a blanket wrapped around her shoulders and the door open beside her.

"Nothing has changed, Al," I said from where I stood outside the car. "You're the same girl you've always been."

"Yeah," she said softly. "But now I know who that is. *What* that is."

"Don't think that this gives you an excuse to ignore your laundry and grow science experiments in the bathroom. Saying 'the devil made me do it' isn't going to fly as an excuse, young lady."

As I'd hoped, she laughed. But the sparkle faded quickly. "We need to talk, Mom."

"I know."

"And I need to talk to Daddy."

"I know that too."

"But not now. Please, can I just pretend that part never happened? Not for forever. Just until we get back home. I just—I just want to be me a little while longer."

"Oh baby," I said, crouching just outside the car and holding tight to her hands. "You'll never be anyone else. But yes. I think it's time to slide into real vacation-mode, don't you? Forget everything. Eat pasta. Go all-out with the tourist stuff. Okay?"

She nodded. "Considering everything, I *totally* think I deserve a massive shopping spree." She smiled then, and I almost melted with relief when I saw the sparkle in her eye.

"Yeah, sweetheart," I said, overwhelmed by the strength, resilience and, yes, predictability of my teenage daughter. "I think shopping is definitely on the agenda."

I tilted my head to catch Stuart's eye. "Sightseeing, too. What would you think about a day at the *Castel Sant'Angelo*?" I asked as he moved to stand beside me.

"I can't think of anything better," he said, pulling me close.

I thought of Eliza in the hospital. Of Eric getting debriefed by Father Corletti right that moment as Allie and I waited our turn. I thought of everything that had happened and everything that had been revealed.

And yet despite all that, I was content. Yes, there were still some really Big Issues to deal with, not the least of which was huddled in front of me under her blanket. And, yes, I had a new cousin to get acquainted with. And of course there were still badass demons out there, just itching to stir up trouble. Heck, I even had the potential of a second career hanging over my head like a blinking neon sign just waiting for me to make a decision.

But at the moment, none of that mattered. Right now I just needed my family.

The job could wait.

The worry could wait.

And, yes, the demons could wait.

With any luck, they might even wait until tomorrow.

DEMON-HUNTING SOCCER MOM SERIES!

Don't miss any of these titles in this bestselling series that's in development as a major motion picture!

CARPE DEMON: ADVENTURES OF A DEMON-HUNTING SOCCER MOM

"This book, as crammed with events as any suburban mom's calendar, shows you what would happen if Buffy got married and kept her past a secret. It's a hoot." —Charlaine Harris, New York Times bestselling author of the Sookie Stackhouse series

Kate Connor is your average, everyday mom with two kids, a husband, and one very big secret ... she used to be a Demon-Hunter. Now retired, she's more interested in the domestic than the demonic. So when she catches sight of a demon in Wal-Mart, she tells herself it's some other Hunter's problem. But when that demon attacks her in her kitchen, retirement is no longer an option.

Now Kate has to kick a little demon butt, figure out why the creatures are trying to take her out and take over her home town, and at the same time take care of her 2 year old, deal with a hormonal 14 year old, and try to keep her past a secret from her daughter and her husband.

She's a little out of practice, but hey ... if she can juggle two kids and an impromptu dinner party, ridding the town of demons should be a piece of cake. Like the saying goes, Carpe Demon ... and Kate intends to do just that.

CALIFORNIA DEMON: THE SECRET LIFE OF A DEMON-HUNTING SOCCER MOM

"Ninety-nine percent of the wives and moms in the country will identify with this heroine. I mean, like who hasn't had to battle demons between car pools and play dates?" —Jayne Ann Krentz, New York Times bestselling author

After fourteen years as a stay-at-home mom, Kate Connor has finally rejoined the workforce. But unlike most working moms, Kate can't rearrange her home obligations to fit the needs of her job. Well, not easily, anyway. And not without a few little white lies.

Because the truth is, no one in her family has any clue that she's returned to the job of her youth. Which means no late nights working beside her husband at the kitchen table while the kids watch television. Although, when you think about it, that's not necessarily a bad thing.

Because when your job is fighting demons, taking your work home with you is a really, really bad idea ...

DEMONS ARE FOREVER: CONFESSIONS OF A DEMON-HUNTING SOCCER MOM

Once again, Kate Connor has a problem. Several, actually.

For one thing, her daughter has figured out that mom is a Demon-Hunter—and wants to be just like her when she grows up.

And there's that nagging suspicion that her dead husband has come back to life in the body of another man. Plus, her living husband still doesn't know her secrets.

Not to mention the fact that she's acquired a mystical item that the entire demon community seems hell-bent on reclaiming.

It's all in a day's work for this stay-at-home mom. But one thing is for certain: sometimes life in the suburbs really can be hell.

DEJA DEMON: THE DAYS AND NIGHTS OF A DEMON-HUNTING SOCCER MOM

Kate Conner is an expert at multi-tasking. Wife, mom, Demon-Hunter. She can stuff hundreds of Easter eggs for the neighborhood fair and still have enough energy to pummel a demon back into the ether.

But Kate's life has gotten more complicated...

Her first husband has returned from the dead in the body of her daughter's chemistry teacher. Different body, same hot desire for Kate. Her daughter now obsesses about becoming a Demon-Hunter the way she used to obsess about boys.

And her current husband is suddenly very suspicious of his wife's extra-domestic activities. What is she doing and who is she doing it with?

And the threat has gotten bigger...

A powerful high demon has returned to San Diablo, seeking not only the key to invincibility, but revenge upon Kate—and Kate's family. And just in case that wasn't trouble enough, there's a new kind of evil in suburbia. The walking dead kind.

And they don't mind making house calls...

DEMON EX MACHINA: TALES OF A DEMON-HUNTING SOCCER MOM

Demon-Hunter Kate Connor is having a very bad month.

Her resurrected first husband houses the soul of a demon.

Her current husband is being overly attentive to the point of smothering.

Her toddler son has entered a tantrum phase.

And her teenage daughter is still determined to be the next, best demon slayer. Worse, she's determined to get her learner's permit the day she turns fifteen.

That's a lot for one woman to juggle, even a Demon-Hunter. Add saving the world to the mix, and things are about to get complicated...

THE DEMON YOU KNOW (A DEMON-HUNTING SOCCER MOM SHORT STORY)

When daughter Allie finds herself knee-deep in demons, Demon Hunter Kate Connor must come to the rescue in this first short story featuring not only Kate, but fourteen year old Allie, too!

PAX DEMONICA: TRIALS OF A DEMON-HUNTING SOCCER MOM

When orphan Kate goes to Rome with her family, she's hoping for a little R&R. The chance to bond with her husband, spend quality time with her kids, and visit her pseudo-family at *Forza Scura*.

In other words, this suburban mom is doing the tourist thing, and intending to do it up right. But while Kate may want to take cheesy pictures and buy overpriced souvenirs, the demon population has other plans. And soon Kate and over-eager daughter Allie are thrust into the middle of a demonic feud.

Now Kate is going to have to call on both her hunting skills and her mothering skills – because if she fails, Kate and family might just find themselves sightseeing in hell.

Visit www.demonhuntingsoccermom.com to learn more!

PLEASE ENJOY THIS
EXCERPT FROM
TAINTED,
BOOK 1 IN JULIE'S BLOOD LILY
CHRONICLES SERIES!

I woke up in total darkness, so out of sorts that I was convinced I'd pulled on the wrong skin along with my blue jeans. Couple that with the fact that anvils were about to split my head wide open, and I think it's fair to say that I wasn't having a good time. I tried to roll over and get my bearings, but even the tiniest movement kicked the hammers in my head to triple-time, and I abandoned the effort before I even got started.

"Fucking A," I said, and immediately wished I hadn't. I'm no American Idol contestant, but my voice doesn't usually inflict extreme pain. Today, it did.

Today? Like I even knew what day it was. Or where I was. Or, for that matter, why I was.

I'd died, after all.

Hadn't I?

Disoriented, I lurched up, only to be halted before I'd barely moved.

I tried again, and realized my wrists and ankles were firmly tied down. What the—?

My heart pounded against my rib cage, but I told myself I wasn't afraid. A big hairy lie, but it was worth a try. I mean, I lied to myself all the time, right? Sometimes I even believed my own shit.

Not this time. I might have dropped out of high school, but I know when to be scared, and tied up in the dark is definitely one of those times. There was no nice, cozy explanation for my current sitch. Instead, my mind filled with high-def NC-17 images of a long, thin blade and a twisted expression of cruel delight painted on a face I knew only too well. Lucas Johnson.

Because this had to be about revenge. Payback for what I'd tried to do. And now I was going to die at the hand of the man I'd gone out to kill.

No, no, no.

No way was I dying. Not now. Not when I'd survived this far.

I didn't have a clue why I was still alive—I remembered the knife; I remembered the blood. But here I was, living and breathing and, yeah, I was a little immobile at the moment, but I was alive. And I intended to stay that way.

No way was I leaving my little sister to the mercy of the son of a bitch who'd raped and brutalized her. Who'd sent her black roses and mailed erotic postcards. All anonymous. All scary as hell. She would see him in stores, lurking around corners, and by the time she screamed for help, he was gone.

The cops had nailed his sorry ass, but when the system had tossed him on a technicality, I watched Rose come close to losing it every single day. I couldn't stand the thought that the system had kicked the monster free when he should have been in a cage, locked away so he couldn't hurt any more little girls. So he couldn't hurt Rose.

So I'd stolen the gun. I'd tracked him down. And God help me, I'd fired.

At the time, I thought I'd hit him square in the chest. But I must have missed, because I could remember Johnson rushing me. After that, things were blurrier. I remembered the terror of knowing that I was dying, and I recalled a warm flood of hope. But I had no clue what had happened between warm, fuzzy hope and the cold, hard slab that made up my current reality.

I peered into the darkness again, and this time the velvet curtain seemed to be lifting. The room, I realized, wasn't completely black. Instead, there was a single candle against the far wall, its small flame gathering strength against the blackness.

I stared, puzzled. I was certain there'd been no flame earlier.

Slowly, the area around me shifted into a reddish gray with dark and light spots contrasting to reveal a line of angular symbols painted above the candlestick.

My eyes locked on the symbols, and the trembling started up again. Something was off, and I was overwhelmed by the frantic, urgent fear that the monster I knew was nowhere nearby, and that when I saw what I was *really* up against, I'd desperately wish it were Johnson's sorry ass that was after me.

A cold chill raced up my spine. I wanted the hell out of there.

I was about to start thrashing again—in the desperate hope that the ties would miraculously loosen—when I heard the metallic screech of a creaking hinge. I froze, my breathing shallow, my muscles tense.

The creak intensified and a shaft of anorexic light swept wide across the room as the door arced open. A huge shadow filled the gap. A dark, monstrous form was silhouetted in the doorway, emitting a scent that made me almost vomit.

A monster. And not of the Lucas Johnson variety.

No, Lucas Johnson was a Boy Scout compared to the putrid creature that lumbered forward, bending so that it could fit through the door frame. It lurched toward me, muscles rolling under an elephant-like hide. The creature wore no clothing, and even in the dark, I could see the parasites living in slime inside the folds of skin. Could hear them scurry for safety when the beast moved toward me.

The fetid smell that preceded it made me gag, and I struggled to sink into the stone slab as the beast peered down at me, a string of snot hanging precariously from the orifice that served as a nose.

The creature's mouth twisted, dry skin cracking as the muscles underneath moved, thin lines of blood and pus oozing out from the newly formed fissures. It swaggered to the candle, then leaned over and breathed on the flame. As if its breath were gas, fire leaped into the air, painting the wall with flame and making the symbols glow.

I cried out in alarm and pain, my body suddenly burning from within—the sensation passing as quickly as it had come.

The beast turned to sneer at me. "You," it croaked. Black piggy eyes lit with fury as it brandished a short, bloodied dagger. "Now we finish this business."

A piercing shriek split the dark, and I realized the sound was coming from me. Fire shot through my limbs, and I jerked upright with a fresh burst of determination. To my surprise and relief, I managed to rip my arms free, the ties flapping from my wrists like useless wings.

The creature paused, drawing itself up to its full height. It took a step backward, then dropped to its knees and held its clawed hands high. With the dagger, it sliced its palm, then let the thick, black liquid that flowed from the wound drip into its open mouth. "I serve the Dark Lord, my Master," it said, the words as rough as tires on gravel. "For my sacrifice, I will be rewarded."

The "sacrifice" thing totally freaked me out, but I took advantage of this quaint little monster ritual to reach down and tear at the ties that still bound my ankles. As I did, I noticed that I was wearing a silky white gown, most definitely not the jeans and T-shirt I'd left the house in.

Not that I had time to mull over such fascinating fashion tidbits. Instead, I focused on the business at hand: getting the hell out of there.

About the time I finished ripping, the creature finished praying. It barreled toward me, dagger outstretched. I rolled over, hiking up the skirt as I kicked up and off the slab to land upright beside it. There's probably a name for a move like that, but I didn't know it. Hell, I didn't even know that my body would move like that.

I didn't waste time savoring my new acrobatic persona; instead, I raced for the door. Or, at least, I started to. The sight of the Hell Beast looming there sort of turned me off that plan. Which left me with no choice but to whip around and try to find another exit.

Naturally, there wasn't one.

No, no, no. So far, I had survived the most screwed-up, freaky day of my life, and I wasn't giving up now. And if that meant I fought the disgusting Hell Beast, then dammit, that was just what I was going to do.

The beast must have had the same idea, because as soon as I turned back toward the door, it lashed out, catching me across the face with the back of its massive, clawed hand. The blow sent me hurtling, and I crashed against the huge brass candlestick, causing it to tumble down hard on my rib cage.

Hot wax burned into my chest, but I had no time to reflect on the pain. The beast was on top of me. I did the only thing I could. I grabbed the stick and thrust it upward. The beast weighed a ton, but I must have had decent leverage, because I managed to catch him under the chin with the stick, knocking his head back and eliciting a howl that almost burst my eardrums.

Not being an idiot, I didn't wait around for him to recover. The candlestick was too heavy to carry as a weapon, so I dropped it and ran like hell toward the door, hoping the beast was alone.

I stumbled over the threshold, never so happy to be in a dark, dank hallway. The only light came from medieval-looking candleholders lining the walls every eight or so feet, but as I wasn't sightseeing, the lack of light didn't bother me much. All I wanted was out of there. So I raced on, down musty corridors and around tight corners until finally—*finally*—I slammed into the push bar of a fire door. An alarm screamed into the night as the thick metal door burst open, and I slid out, my nose crinkling as I caught the nasty smell of rotting food, carried on the cool autumn air. I was in an alley, and as my eyes adjusted, I turned to the right and raced toward the street and the safety of the world.

It wasn't until I reached the intersection of the alley and an unfamiliar street that I paused to turn back. The alley was silent. No monsters. No creatures. No boogeymen out to get me.

The street was silent as well. No people or traffic. The streetlights blinking. Late, I thought. And my next thought was to run some more. I would have, too, if I hadn't looked down and noticed my feet in the yellow glow of the street-lamps.

I blinked, confused. Because those didn't look like my feet. And now that I thought about it, my hands and legs seemed all wrong, too. And the bloom of red I now saw on the breast of the white gown completely freaked me out. Which, when you considered the overall circumstances, was saying a lot. Because on the whole, this experience was way, way, way trippy, and the only thing I could figure was that someone had drugged me and I was in the middle of one monster of a hallucination.

Then again, maybe the simplest explanation was the right one: I was losing my mind.

"You're not."

I spun around and found myself looking down on a squat little man in a green overcoat and a battered brown fedora. At least a head shorter than me, he was looking up at me with eyes that would have been serious were they not so amphibian.

"You're not losing it," the frog-man clarified, which suggested to me that I was. Losing it, I mean. After all, the strange little man had just read my mind.

He snorted. "That doesn't make you crazy. Just human."

"Who the devil are you?" I asked, surprised to find that my voice worked, though it sounded somewhat off. I glanced up and down the street, calculating my odds of getting away. Surely I could run faster than this—

"No need to run," he said. Then he stepped off the sidewalk and into the street. As if it had been waiting for his cue, a sleek black limousine pulled to the curb. Frog-man opened the rear door and nodded. "Hop in."

I took a step backward. "Get lost, dickwad."

"Come on, kid. We need to talk. And I know you must be tired. You've had a hell of a day." He nodded down the alley. "You did good in there. But next time remember that you're supposed to kill them. Not give 'em a headache. *Capisce?*"

I most definitely did *not capisce*. "Next time?" I pointed back down the alley. "You had something to do with that? No way," I said, taking another step backward. "No freaking way."

"It's a lot to take in, I know." He opened the door wider. "Why don't you get in, Lily? We really should talk."

My name echoed through the night I looked around, wary, but there was no one else around. "I want answers, you son of a bitch."

He shook his head, and I could imagine him muttering, *tsk*, *tsk*. "Hard to believe you're the one all the fuss is about, but the big guy must know what he's doing, right?"

I blinked.

"But look at you, staring at me like I'm talking in Akkadian. To you I probably am. You're exhausted, right? I tell you, jumping right into the testing . . . it's just not the best method." He shook his head, and this time the *tsk*, *tsk* actually emerged. "But do they ask me? No. I mean, who am I? Just old Clarence, always around to help. It's enough to give a guy an inferiority complex." He patted my shoulder, making contact before I could pull away. "Don't you worry. This can all wait until tomorrow."

"What testing? What's tomorrow? And who are you?"

"All in good time. Right now," he said, "I'm taking you home."

And before I could ask how he planned to manage that, because I had no intention of getting into the limo with him, he reached over and tapped me on the forehead. "Go to sleep, pet. You need the rest."

I wanted to protest, but couldn't. My eyes closed, and the last thing I remember was his amphibian grin as my knees gave out and I fell to the sidewalk at the frog-man's feet.

ABOUT JULIE

A *New York Times, USA Today, Publishers Weekly*, and *Wall Street Journal* bestselling author, Julie Kenner (aka J. Kenner) writes a range of stories including romance (erotic, sexy, funny & sweet), young adult novels, chick lit suspense and paranormal mommy lit. Her foray into the latter, *Carpe Demon: Adventures of a Demon-Hunting Soccer Mom*, was selected as a Booksense Summer Paperback Pick for 2005, was a Target Breakout Book, was a Barnes & Noble Number One SFF/Fantasy bestseller for seven weeks, and is in development as a feature film with 1492 Pictures.

As J. Kenner, she also writes erotic romance (including the bestselling Stark Trilogy) as well as dark and sexy paranormal romances, including the Shadow Keeper series previously published as J.K. Beck.

You can connect with Julie through her website,
www.juliekenner.com,
Twitter (@juliekenner)
and her Facebook pages at
www.facebook.com/juliekennerbooks and
www.facebook.com/jkennerbooks.

For all the news on upcoming releases, contests, and other fun stuff, be sure to sign up for her newsletter.